No! It can't be!
Not the Capriati Curse!

All Ben's life he'd seen the effect of this ridiculous curse on the men in his family. In 150 years none had escaped their fate—to fall in love with their exact opposite, and remain hopelessly in love for the rest of their lives.

Capriati men lost their heads and any semblance of control when they lost their heart. And Ben vowed that his would stay intact, thank you very much. If this instant attraction was the Curse acting on him, he'd fight destiny with a smile, defy fate with a laugh.

He grinned devilishly at Lucy Miles as she stood angrily on the doorstep, eager to claim his—her—their?—sweepstakes prizes. "Then I guess it's showdown or standoff, Miss Miles. We'll just have to find out if this house is big enough for the both of us."

Dear Reader,

In this month of tricks or treats, there's no magic to delivering must-read love stories each month. We simply publish upbeat stories from the heart and hope you find them a treat.

What can you do to keep these great stories coming? Plenty! You can write me or visit our online community at www.eHarlequin.com and let me know the stories you like best. Or if you have trouble finding the latest Silhouette Romance titles, be sure to remind your local bookseller how much you enjoy them. This way you will never miss your favorites.

For example, IN A FAIRY TALE WORLD... combines classic love stories, a matchmaking princess and a sprinkling of fairy-tale magic for all-out fun! Myrna Mackenzie launches this Silhouette Romance six-book series with *Their Little Cowgirl* (#1738)—the story of a cowboy and urban Cinderella who lock horns and then hearts over his darling baby daughter.

In *Georgia Gets Her Groom!* (#1739), the latest in Carolyn Zane's THE BRUBAKER BRIDES series, Georgia discovers that Mr. Wrong might be the right man for her, after all. Then watch what happens when a waitress learns her new ranch hand is a tycoon in disguise, in *The Billionaire's Wedding Masquerade* (#1740) by Melissa McClone. And if you like feisty heroines and the wealthy heroes that sweep them off their feet, you'll want to read *Cinderella's Lucky Ticket* by Melissa James (#1741).

Read these romance treats and share the love and laughter with Silhouette Romance this month!

Mavis C. Allen
Associate Senior Editor, Silhouette Romance

Please address questions and book requests to:
Silhouette Reader Service
U.S.: 3010 Walden Ave., P.O. Box 1325, Buffalo, NY 14269
Canadian: P.O. Box 609, Fort Erie, Ont. L2A 5X3

Cinderella's Lucky Ticket

MELISSA JAMES

SILHOUETTE *Romance*®

Published by Silhouette Books

America's Publisher of Contemporary Romance

This book is for Katie, who suggested the plot;
and long overdue thanks to Barbara and Peter Clendon,
without whose knowledge (and magnificent contest)
I wouldn't have been able to write this dedication.
Thanks, as always to All of Us—you know why;
and to Maryanne and Diane, for being there…again.

SILHOUETTE BOOKS

ISBN 0-373-19741-1

CINDERELLA'S LUCKY TICKET

Copyright © 2004 by Lisa Chaplin

Visit Silhouette Books at www.eHarlequin.com

Printed in U.S.A.

MELISSA JAMES

is a mother of three living in a beach suburb in county New South Wales. A former nurse, waitress, store assistant, perfume and chocolate (yum!) demonstrator among other things, she believes in taking on new jobs for the fun experience. She'll try almost anything at least once to see what it feels like—a fact that scares her family on regular occasions. She fell into writing by accident when her husband brought home an article stating how much a famous romance author earned, and she thought, "I can do that!" Years later, she found her niche at Silhouette Intimate Moments. Currently writing a pilot/spy series set in the South Pacific, she can be found most mornings walking and swimming at her local beach with her husband, or every afternoon running around to her kids' sporting hobbies, while dreaming of flying, scuba diving, belaying down a cave or over a cliff—anywhere her characters are at the time!

Come and make all your fantasies come true.

PLAY the

Lakelands

Children's Charities Sweepstakes!

**You could be set for life with this
fabulous grand prize — a waterfront house on
Queensland's gorgeous Gold Coast!**

The lucky grand-prize winner will also get two luxury cars,
a new boat and an exotic holiday in beautiful Bali—
so come and play today!
Buying a ticket can change your life—
so what are you waiting for?

Prologue

Trapani, Sicily, 1853

"Look at him, Patrizia," one woman commented to her neighbor over coffee, pointing at the object of her disgust: a young man sauntering down the cobbled road with a group of his friends. "He walks—no, he *swaggers*. Like one who knows he will have all the girls clamoring for his attention tonight. He thinks he is the most handsome, charming young man in all of Sicily."

"Well, perhaps he has reason, Anna." Patrizia smiled with indulgent patience, watching the man-child strutting down the road as if he were a conquering emperor. "He looks like a statue of Apollo I saw once in Rome, when I was a girl. Those Capriati boys are too handsome and charming for their own good! I remember his father at that age…ah, for Vincenzo, my heart would flutter…"

"Yes," Anna muttered, her voice dark, "Enzo was a handsome devil, and just as bigheaded. They are all alike, these

Capriatis. But one day, their arrogance and their careless ways with the local girls will come back to haunt them, mark my words."

A shadow crossed the sun at that moment, though no clouds littered the afternoon sky. "Alleluia," both women muttered with a shudder, crossing themselves.

"*Giovanni Capriati!*" The strident cry rang across the street clear to the public square at one end, which was filled with flowers and bright-colored banners for tonight's May Day dance for the young people. "*Giovanni Capriati!*"

The women gasped. That fiery voice could not be mistaken—it was Sophia Morelli, the local witch. Her heart's treasure, her silly, pretty teenage daughter Giulia stood half-crouched behind her, sobbing.

So Anna's prophecy was having an immediate fulfillment...and this time, not only Anna and Patrizia crossed themselves.

Yet the Capriati boy did not so much as turn his head, but he continued strutting down the road, laughing with his friends.

"Giovanni Capriati, you will stop! You will listen to me!"

With the little, careless shrug that only a Capriati could accomplish the boy turned, his dark, so-handsome-it-was-almost-pretty face bored. "Yes, Signorina Morelli? May I assist you?"

"You broke my daughter's heart!" the famed wisewoman cried, her face scorched with the heat of livid fury. "Do you deny you met her in secret, kissed her, promised her your love and then moved on to the next girl?"

"I only kissed her! What's the harm in that? I promised Giulia nothing, woman," Giovanni retorted, his head high, eyes bland. "I have never done so with any girl. I am not an idiot, to make promises to a witch's get," he muttered to his friends. The boys laughed, nudging each other.

"I heard that, *ragazzo!*" Sophia's voice rang to the rafters of each house. Within moments the windows filled with avid faces, enjoying the rare sight of someone standing up to Sophia, who knew herb lore and was rumored to have poisoned her first husband when he was unfaithful. "Now, you will pay for crossing me!"

A teary whimper came from behind her. "No, Mama, no…do not kill him! Do not hurt him! Think what you do!"

Sophia's face, still holding a haughty loveliness at fifty, smiled at her distraught daughter. "I think of you, and the boy's papa who broke my sister's heart. The arrogant Capriati men need a lesson…" Her eyes flashed with magnificent fury as she threw down a little sack of herbs and flowers at the boy's feet. "Listen, people of Trapani! You are my witnesses. I curse the Capriati men! From this day they will fall in love with women who are their complete opposites and would have nothing to do with them. For all their charm, they will discover what it is to fight for love!" She chuckled. "And they will not suspect they have met their Fate until it is too late…."

Giovanni looked around at his squirming friends with a careless grin. "This is a *curse?* Woman, you're losing your touch. I thought you capable of better. As if any girl would refuse me!"

Sophia smiled and turned her daughter away from the boy the girl still adored. "You will see, arrogant bambino," she chuckled softly. "*Arrivederci* to your heart, young fool. You will see."

Chapter One

If it weren't for the monkeys, she'd never have dreamed of doing it. But there they were as usual, loud and smelly, spoiled and *loved*. The collective set of final straws that broke her own particular camel's back, and changed her life.

Leaning in the doorway of the laboratory, Abigail Lucinda Miles felt the usual rush of frustrated sorrow. Of course he was still in his crumpled lab coat, leaning over his cage of beloved chimpanzees. "Hugh. You're not ready."

Her fiancé started, spilling his eyedropper onto the petri dish. He turned to her, his tanned, handsome face and brilliant blue eyes cool with displeasure. "You do remember that this experiment is *vital,* and every vial of scent costs hundreds of dollars?"

She sighed, digging her hands into her pockets. "Yes, I know, Hugh, but we're meeting our parents in an hour at Bringelly's to discuss the wedding…"

He added another cautious drop to the clear dish, his blond hair glinting in the light, like a Nordic god. "What—?" Then he sighed. "Oh, yes. I forgot. Can you hold them off an hour or two?"

"I don't think they'll mind," she replied, but couldn't hold in the weary smile.

The chimps jumped up and down in their series of connected cages, screaming, cackling. He swiveled back to his simian friends, his eyes on fire with eagerness. "You like that one, babies?" But seeing no sign of his long-expected reaction, he sighed. "It's just another few months, then we can do other things." He grabbed her shoulders, his eyes blazing. "Abigail, we're so close. With one breakthrough we'd get the corporate funding we need, and I could move on to—"

"Getting married?" she asked, in wistful hope.

"Have I been neglecting you again?" He kissed her nose. "I thought you understood why I've had to concentrate on this the past few months. Sorry, baby. I'll take Saturday off and devote the day to our wedding."

"Really?" Her eyes lit up. "I'll show you my dress. It's white tulle, with a lovely tiara—and I found a great florist—"

"No wonder you're feisty today." His hands fell on her shoulders, breaking into her dreamworld with tender impatience. "Honestly, you scare me at times. You change as swiftly as Jekyll and Hyde. You're on that Lucy kick again."

Sizzling color raced up her cheeks. "Well, it is my name—well, my middle name. Abigail Lucinda Miles." She would *not* give in to the sneaking shame she felt every time her parents or Hugh chided her about her "Lucy kick"—she wouldn't!

He smiled at her over his goggles. "But it doesn't suit you. My Abigail is quiet, modest, *sensible*—just like you are. But when you get on that Lucy kick, you're illogical and wild, wanting silly things. I *know* what's right for us, snooky. A small, simple at-home wedding with no tizzy dress or fuss, and funnel our efforts and funds into the experiment for now." He smiled, winked and slapped her rear. "You can be sure I'll be at the church on time."

"We're not having a church," she muttered. "I don't like organized religion. Do you *know* that about me, Hugh? Do you see *me* at all anymore?"

"Mmm, hmm." Jotting down notes on the chimps' reaction to the latest scent, he didn't look up.

Sudden tears stung her eyes. "Hugh, do you really want to marry *me,* or is it because I'm Professor Miles' daughter?"

"Hold on a tick, sweetie, just finishing these notes…" Hugh scribbled a little more, then he looked up with a slightly harassed smile. "Now what was that?"

Lowering her face to hide her confusion and sorrow, she shook her head and said the words he expected, needed her to say right now. "Nothing, Hugh. It's not important."

His voice filled with warm approval. "Good girl. I know it's hard now, but we'll take a late honeymoon when I've completed my experiment. We'll go anywhere you want once I hit the big time."

She shuffled her toe against the bench, and the words popped out against her will. "If you'd supported me when I wanted funding for my theory on organic growing of apples in arid areas, we could have enough money by now to—"

He sighed as he worked on a new scent. "I've told you a dozen times, baby, your idea isn't feasible. You're a librarian. A perfect scientist's wife-to-be, quiet and supportive." He gave her that quick, *I-wish-you'd-go-now-I'm-busy* look. "Now I really need to get back to work, all right?"

A chimp squealed. Hugh swung around, eyes blazing beneath the goggles, and started scribbling down data on the scent he'd just used. "Yes! Yes…the combination of high floral with the…"

She was invisible again. She could stand in front of him and he'd see through her, right to those petted, spoiled monkeys…

A minute later she trudged down the street to her car in the warmth of the spring evening, kicking rocks. "Is it so much to ask, to have him participate in our wedding day?" *Lovely gardens and horse-drawn carriages, lace and tulle and orange blossom…* Lost in dreams, she sighed. Right now, she'd settle for Hugh just waiting for her at the end of the aisle without a petri dish or a cage of chimps to distract him.

You'll never have it—Abigail, an inner imp mocked. *You're doomed to go from neglected child to forgotten wife. You've lived on campus since birth. You don't know anyone, and nothing about the world apart from theory and thesis. You've never been outside Sydney, barely away from the university. Face it, you've got nowhere else to go.*

She kicked another rock. "If I'd got my apple experiment I'd have something besides the wedding to concentrate on. I'd have *my* wedding…and if I funded his experiment I'd get Hugh's attention…."

Her mother's words of last week drifted into her mind, in that cool, lecturing tone that always made her feel so childish and selfish. "His work is *vital,* Abigail. Don't get so worked up about things that don't matter in the overall scheme of things. Hugh's research helps humanity for life. Try not to think of yourself all the time, dear. It's only a wedding. He'll marry you one day. Surely you can wait a few more months…or a year?"

W-well…of course she could, she'd done it before, but—but it was so *embarrassing* to have to cancel the wedding again….

She sighed, climbed into her old coupe and turned on the radio, letting the easy-listening music soothe her. Her eyes closed; her head fell back on the seat. "I'm better now. I'm fine. I'm happy." The mantra of her mother's analyst helped the panic subside. She drove home to her one-room flat, tidying her messy bun, reapplying lipstick, buttoning up her cardigan at each set of red lights. "What's wrong with a simple wedding, and taking a honeymoon when his experiment's complete?" She turned into the driveway, winking foolish tears away. "We'll have a second wedding when he makes the big time...."

Try if, *Abigail,* that horrible inner imp mocked. *Six years and he's still no closer to his dream...and neither are you.*

"Stop it. Stop it!" She shook her head to clear it, and yanked open the mailbox.

At least that brought her a little gift. Oh, joy...a fat envelope with a big, glossy sweepstakes brochure inside. She gave a whoop of delight. Reading these brochures, dreaming of winning, was her secret fantasy—a harmless double life Hugh and her parents knew nothing about. With a smile of mingled anticipation and guilty pleasure, she ripped it open.

"Congratulations to Ben Capriati, the winner of Lakelands Children's Charities Sweepstakes Draw 224! Here's Ben outside his grand prize, a lovely waterfront home on Queensland's sparkling Gold Coast. Having bought the hundred-dollar option book of tickets, Ben also won two luxury cars, a boat and a Bali holiday...."

She gazed at the dark, brawny, raffishly smiling man in the black leather jacket, jeans and work boots. Lucky Ben Capriati. Even rough-riding bikers had their dreams come true.

Lucky Ben's lady. A beautiful home, two cars, a boat and a dark, rugged man who wouldn't forget to take her to dinner if she stopped putting monthly reminders on the calendar....

She gasped at that renegade imp taking over her mind. "Stop it. Stop it!" She read on, refusing to look at the handsome jerk with the five o'clock shadow, concentrating on the prizes he'd won. "...with ticket number...huh?" Grabbing her ticket from her purse, she checked the ticket number against hers. "What? But—but surely that's—" She snatched up the brochure, her amazed, hungry gaze taking in the winning-ticket number, and her own. *"He won?"* she cried. "It's…mine! He. Won. With *my* ticket!"

Minchin Hills, Gold Coast, Queensland

Another day in paradise…

Ben Capriati let himself in the back door of his gorgeous home, sweating from a midmorning barefoot run on the sandy shores of his exclusive beachfront neighborhood. Time for a lazy dip in the resort-style pool, then maybe he'd do lunch by the beach. Ah, Queensland, the glorious Sunshine State! Nine hundred kilometers north of Sydney, but a million miles from his regular life.

He'd promised himself a vacation throughout all his years of university and medical school, working two jobs to get through, and then those long, frenetic shifts at the inner-city hospital in Sydney as an intern and then resident doctor. And now, he was finally free to begin his life and profession—and this was the perfect start, a refreshing week or two before he left for the hot, dusty town of Monilough, and the Outback practice awaiting him in northwestern New South Wales.

Fun and games for one glorious week, sun and heat and *Baywatch*-type babes strolling beneath a blazing clear sky, getting a tan before his eyes. And at the end of the vacation he'd sell the lot, and buy a house in the Outback town he'd signed up to help.

Now, he had the world on a string. For the first time in his life he had something wonderful all his own without working his butt off to get it, and nobody could take it from him.

Meanwhile, the pool calls! He stripped off his T-shirt and grabbed a towel.

Rap-rap-rap. *Bang-bang-BANG!*

He swiveled around at the aggressive belting at his door. It wasn't a neighbor; in upscale Minchin Hills, the residents were too elegant, too refined to be so loud—or too worried about what the neighbors would think. So he faced the inescapable conclusion. *Uh-oh. They found me…*

A second thunderous knock jolted the house, making the door shudder. He stalked over and pulled the door half-open, rolling his eyes. *Here we go!* "I was wondering when you'd show up—"

"To claim *my* prize, you mean? You *thief!*"

Hmm. That gorgeous, breathy voice definitely didn't belong to any member of his rowdy family. But—*a thief?* He opened the door the whole way, looked at the speaker and blinked again.

No *way!*

This mousy, cardigan-clad little drudge owned the sexy Marilyn voice? He couldn't begin to guess her age with the grotesque dark shades hiding her face—not to mention the outfit. Yikes, bright green culottes and a fuzzy pink cardigan—and with that bundled-up bun, she could be a refugee from that seventies show his sister Sofie liked. Or was it *The Fly?* The tortoiseshell shades certainly gave her a bug-eyed look, all right.

"I'm so sorry to interrupt you…"

He dragged his attention to the voice in the background. A harassed, anxious, middle-aged man in a brown suit stood behind the woman, wringing his hands.

Ben said mildly, "May I ask what this is about?"

Hanging onto a musty tartan suitcase as if it was her only friend, the cardigan lady pushed past him, marched through the entry, plopped the case down and flung herself on his sofa…but by the simple act of nervously chewing on her thumbnail, she ruined the effect of her belligerent performance.

Ben's eyebrows rose, checking out the suitcase, thrown between them as if it was a gauntlet. Well, given its dust, mold and moth holes, it could have come from the same bygone era.

The harassed suit-man wrung his hands again. "Please, Miss Miles, if you'll only wait till we sort this out—"

The time-warp lady stopped chewing her finger, pulled off her shades and squared her shoulders, as if for courage—and her messy bun disintegrated. Trails of glossy, dark, twisting curls fell around her face—and she seemed to grow younger, prettier, before his bemused gaze. "Sure." Her breathy voice brushed past Ben's ears with a wickedly sexy effect. "I'll, um, just wait *here* until you sort it out."

Ben leaned on the doorpost in deep, quiet enjoyment, watching the queer pageant unfold before him—the nervous wreck in the doorway, and Mighty Mouse on his sofa. "Can I help you?"

"Yes. You can." The aforesaid mouse glared at him with indignant blue eyes, her creamy face flushed and rosy. Yeah, she was young all right, and like no drudge he'd ever seen—more like a babe in hiding. "You can get out of *my* house!"

His eyebrows shot up. O-okay. This gal needed a diagnosis, and fast. She'd focused her anger onto a complete stranger—and she'd called him a thief. Paranoid delusions? "Sorry, Miss—Miles, was it? I think you've made a mistake."

"*I* didn't make a mistake." She pointed with a stabbing motion at the suit-man. "*They* gave you *my* ticket!"

His gaze followed the accusatory finger. "Ticket?" he asked of the suit-man, hoping for a sensible answer, since the cutie in the cardigan appeared to be in severe need of Prozac—no, Xanax. She needed calming down…yeah, if she got her hands on any uppers right now she'd ruin his chance at future fatherhood.

The man smiled in half-cringing apology. "Mr. Capriati,

do you remember me? I'm Ken Hill, director of Lakelands Children's Charities Sweepstakes Draw—"

"Of course! I thought I knew your face." Ben stepped forward to shake hands. "What's this about my ticket?"

"*My* ticket!"

He swiveled back to meet her glare head-on—and then he couldn't tear his gaze away. Maybe it was the wild dark curls cascading around her waiflike face in such sweet disarray, or the pink-lipped half pout, all but begging to be kissed. "Fine, your ticket," he agreed, to placate her.

She smiled in triumph at Mr. Hill. "See? He admits it!"

"Whoa." He lifted a hand. "I don't admit to anything until I know what I'm admitting to."

She tossed her head. "You stole my prizes!"

"Uh-huh." He tried not to grin. This gal was nuts! Cute, but nuts. "Can you explain how I managed that when we've never even met?"

"Okay, it's his fault!" She pointed at Mr. Hill who still stood dithering in the entryway.

"Well, um—" Mr. Hill stammered, "it seems there's been some confusion with the winning ticket in your draw, Mr. Capriati. It appears you and Miss Miles received the same numbered ticket."

"It's *my* ticket!"

Ben smiled, trying to soothe her. "How about we let Mr. Hill tell his story before we fight over whose ticket it is?"

Mr. Hill's wrinkled face lightened, looking intensely grateful for the intervention. "We've been experiencing, ah, technical difficulties with the system of ticket distribution—"

Cardigan Cutie jumped in again. "What he *means* is their lawyer embezzled all the money set aside for new computers, and the system crashed the day they made up our tickets."

"Uh-huh. Go on, Mr. Hill," he murmured.

Mr. Hill sighed. "Unfortunately, Miss Miles is right. Our computers have now been replaced, but the day we sent out your tickets the old computers glitched, and sent out two copies each of twelve sets of tickets, but with different names on each set. The glitch affected the winning ticket, plus the one-off prizes. At the moment, we're unsure to which of you the win belongs. Miss Miles came to our office this morning—"

"Threatening litigation," she said. How did she manage to sound smug, breathless, nervous, exhilarated and terrified at once? "They didn't notify *me* about the mix-up. They hoped I'd never find out!" She lifted an eyebrow as Mr. Hill squirmed. "W-well?"

Ben looked into her eyes. *Calm her down, or there's no telling what she'll do next!* "Can we please let Mr. Hill finish what he's got to say first?"

The girl tossed her head, her face mutinous...and this time he couldn't hold back the grin. Flying dark curls, roses-and-cream skin, pouty mouth, big, scornful Irish eyes and a sinful whisky voice against a crazy circus getup. Man, she was right out of the ordinary—and her apparent addiction to possessive italics only added to her unconscious appeal. With the right outfit, she'd hit the big-time honey league—and if she'd shown up for any other reason, he might've helped her to discover the fact. As a lifetime connoisseur of good-looking women—but only in the past seven years when he found a spare minute or two—he'd rate this one at least a 9, maybe 9.5 out of 10. Apart from the charity-bin duds, of course.

"Um," Mr. Hill went on, "since this has no precedent, I explained to Miss Miles that we'll need time to sort out the legalities. But she insisted on coming to the house—"

"Or I'd take it to the media." She looked absurdly pleased with her inventiveness, like a little girl who'd pushed a chair to the cookie jar. "The ticket's as much mine as yours. These prizes should be mine. So here I am—here I stay—and you can't make me go. Possession is nine-tenths of the law." She looked at him in defiant, half-scared challenge, as if she'd surprised even herself with her own audacity. As if she'd scooped up a dozen cookies in her hands already, and expected him to snatch them away from her any second.

That was it. He was gone. Ben's mouth twitched once, then again, before he gave in and burst out laughing.

She jerked up on the sofa and clutched the sides of her cardigan together, gaping at him in the most comic, kissable indignation he'd ever seen. "You're *laughing* at me?"

"Can't—can't—" He doubled over, hanging on to the wall for balance, his stomach hurting with the uncontrollable gusts of laughter. He couldn't figure out if she belonged in a museum or an asylum. "You're a riot, babe. A five-foot-two cardigan-clad home invader, and *I can't make you go?*"

A shudder ran through her. "Don't patronize me, Capriati—" his name spoken in total distaste "—and don't call me *babe*. It's a demeaning term designed to relegate women to sexual objects."

"Okay, Miss Miles," he laughed, amused by her indignation, and her dislike of him—meeting a woman less than eager to please was a rare thing for him. "I agree possession is nine-tenths of the law—but you've missed a vital point. With myself also in possession, you only have four and a half of those nine…and since *I* possess the keys I can pick you up, dump you on the doorstep and retain my nine without a hassle."

She gasped, jumped to her feet and pointed at him like a lawyer in court. "Try it, you ignorant ape. I'll sue you for assault. With Mr. Hill to act as witness in court for me—" Mr. Hill visibly paled at her words, and edged toward the door "—I'll get everything!"

Oh, man, *this* was an even better way to spend a vacation!

A challenge, a crazy scenario, and a smart, pretty, slightly off-the-wall girl who wanted to beat him instead of winning him over. Yeah, this was gonna be *fun!* Aiming to rile her, he winked. "Go for it. I dare you to try."

"Try? I'll win. I'll win the lot!" She stood quivering before him, flushed with fury, her lovely eyes shooting sparks at him. She was so spitting-mad *sweet* he wanted to scoop her up against him and pet her until she purred....

Something inside him skidded to a shocked halt. What was going on here? Why wasn't he furious at this unannounced invasion of his house? This feeling of utter delight at the prospect of spending a few days with her—even if she gadded about in those trailer-park-reject duds—was completely insane.

Ben was a guy who usually went with his gut instinct—he had to in his career, it often saved lives—but this whole scenario was too weird to trust. Somehow it felt as if this girl, this Miss Miles, was meant to come here to him. As if it was—fate, kismet, serendipity. Or—

Oh, no. It can't be! Not the Capriati Curse!

All his life he'd seen the effect of this ridiculous Curse on the men in his family. In a hundred and fifty years none had beaten the fate laid down by the furious Sicilian wisewoman. Her daughter's broken heart led her to place the Curse upon his careless, flirtatious great-great-great-grandfather, who'd ended up falling madly in love with a shy, stuttering girl who'd made him wait for her for seven agonizing years while she nursed her sick mother before she'd marry him.

Not that he'd cared. For when a Capriati man loved, the woman was always an absolute opposite to him, yet he remained hopelessly in love for the rest of his life.

It had even happened to Papa. Mama had been his fiancée's bridesmaid-to-be. He'd met her only at the wedding rehearsal two days before the wedding. The very public furor created by that case of Capriati love made him shudder, every time he thought about it.

In fact, *every* case of Capriati love made him shudder in absolute horror. Capriati men lost their heads and any semblance of control over their lives whenever they lost their heart. His was staying intact, thank you very much.

No way. No way! This Curse will not happen to me—and it definitely won't be with a stitched-up lunatic like this one!

No *way*. If this was the Curse acting on him, he'd fight destiny with a smile, and defy fate with a laugh. "Then I guess it's showdown, or standoff, Miss Miles. We'll just have to find out if this house is big enough for both of us."

Chapter Two

"You think this is a *joke?*"

She gaped at him in total incredulity. This half-naked crazy Neanderthal was all but rolling on the pristine white carpet in laughter. He was *laughing* at this situation? "What sort of idiot thinks losing half a million dollars is funny?"

The infuriating ape straightened up, leaned back on the wall and folded his arms over the muscles of his bare chest, wearing a big, dimpled Cheshire-cat grin. "Life's too short to get uptight. And since I plan on winning this race, I might as well enjoy the ride to the finish line."

She gulped. Throwback to a lower stage of evolution he might be, but with his lithe build, bronzed skin, careless dark hair flopped over his forehead and deep, dark eyes that twinkled…well, even in her prejudiced view, Ben Capriati could speed up the average female pulse without trying. There was something so lush and Mediterranean, so inherently *sensuous* about him a woman couldn't help but respond to—

Other women, not me! I'm far too intelligent to—

"No comeback? Given your ingenuity in getting in here, I thought you'd be a worthier opponent." After a moment he added, "You need help? I can always rile you into a reply—babe."

"You're—you're crude." As crude as George of the Jungle— and every bit as gorgeous, even wearing running shorts instead of a loincloth. Something about him oozed raw sexuality…

So don't look! I'm not here to do anything but take his prizes or some of them. Just enough to fund the wedding. He's standing in the way of my story-book wedding to my perfect man.

"Amateur," he taunted, without malice. "Come on, I'm waiting. Go for it. Hit me with your best shot."

"We'll—we'll see about that!" She studiously kept her eyes above the neck, feeling like a Peeping Tom.

Mr. Hill edged nearer to the door. "Then, Mr. Capriati, if you have no objection to Miss Miles residing here—"

"He has no legal right to object! Does he?" she asked in sudden, confused anxiety. "I mean, if it's my ticket, too—"

"Hey, no objections from me." The ape leaned farther into the wall of the entry to the living room, lazy amusement in every feature. He didn't seem in the least worried by her presence or threats. "Would I object to such gorgeous, charming company?"

"Oh, typical," she muttered, squashing the twinge of hurt. No man ever had, or ever would, call her gorgeous….

"Typical of what?" He slanted her a rakish, wicked grin as she floundered, deriving great enjoyment from her dilemma. "Of?"

She drew a breath, garnered up her courage and said it. "Of—of modern-day proof that the reversion to the caveman Neanderthal isn't yet extinct, but alive and well in the male population!"

He grinned at her, as if her insult didn't bother him in the least. "According to leading anthropologists and paleontologists, Neanderthals were pretty sophisticated dudes, hut dwellers and toolmakers living prior to the Pleistocene era—most modern man as we know it. Grunting, women-dragging cavemen are considered to be more in line with an earlier period, possibly the Paleolithic. Correct me if I'm wrong."

Her jaw almost hit the ground. "How did *you* know—?"

"Let's say I subscribe to the occasional scientific journal when I'm desperate for entertainment." His grin slanted sideways, charming and raffish as a Hollywood buccaneer. "Look, Miss—no, that's ridiculous. If we're going to cohabit for the next week or so and exchange mutually satisfying insults, we can at least drop the mister-miss farce. What's your name?"

She froze. "My—my name?"

"Yeah, your name. Like mine's Ben? You know—Miss, fill-in-the-blank, Miles." His hands made typing gestures. "The thing other people call you, and you answer to. The semiunique title that stops me from yelling, 'Hey, lady!', and half the adult population of Southeastern Queensland from turning around."

"Do—do you think—" The half-guilty temptation overcame the prompting of her conscience. *What does it matter? He'll be out of my life in a few days.* She peeped at him in wistful appeal. "Do you think you could call me Lucy?"

Both eyebrows lifted. "Do I *think* I could call you Lucy? Is it your name, or isn't it?"

Sensing defeat, she sighed. "Well, my real name is Abigail—Abigail Lucinda Miles—so everyone calls me Abigail. It's a quiet, sensible, modest name, like me, but—but I don't like it. I'd love for somebody to call me Lucy, just once," she murmured wistfully.

"Um, right." To her surprise, he chuckled again. "Well,

sorry to disagree with the apparent powers that be, but so fa
based on our short acquaintance, *sensible, quiet and mode*
are the last terms I'd think of in connection with you."

A mixture of total disbelief and pure joy budded to a flowe
of hope inside her. "Then you'll call me Lucy?"

"Sure," he agreed, with a cheerful air. "I like it. Lucy
more your speed than Abigail—at least once the hair's dow
and the cardigan's skew-wif, like it is now."

"That's what *I* think! But—" Then she gasped. "My…hair
My cardigan?" She rushed to the mirror over the hall stand
and saw her hair in a tumbled mess and her cardigan slippin
from one shoulder, leaving it almost bare. "Oh, dear, it's a
the fuss and upset. I need to calm down, do my positive a
firm—" She slammed her mouth shut, concentrating on tid
ing the mess she was in. "Much better. I'm fine. I'm happy.
feel settled, and—" She turned back, satisfied, to see the ap
watching her, containing his obvious amusement. "What a
you laughing at *now?*"

"Whoever the fool was that thought you sensible or quiet
He shook his head. "What sort of jerks are you hangin
around?"

She bristled. "They're not jerks. *My* family are highly re
spected members of the scientific community! Mother is
professor of biology, Father is an endocrinologist, and Hug
my fiancé, is a geneticist!"

His eyebrows lifted. "How intimidating of them."

Tossing her hair in defiance of his flippant attitude, sh
snapped, "I'm proud to be part of a scientific family. I'm
scientific librarian myself. I catalog and store some of th
most important work ever done in this country!"

"I see." His voice quivered. "No wonder you're proud
yourself. That's very, um, impressive."

Stealing another peek at him, she saw that he didn't loc

impressed in the least—more as if he was getting a huge kick out of every word she said. His dark eyes were alight with laughter; his big, bronzed, well-defined and dark-haired chest above his flat, hard stomach, shook with the effort of repressing his glee.

What was she doing, noticing his *chest*—that strong, olive-brown, muscular chest with enough dark springing hair to beg a woman to curl her fingers through it….

Oh, dear. *Houston, we have a problem!*

And she knew just what it was. She'd studied this well-known scientific effect on the feminine psyche for a thesis four years ago. The instinctive reaction to a tall, dark, strong-chested man: the type who could fight off invaders, hunt, provide for his woman, rescue his children from danger. This—this *thing* that had just happened to her was based on pheromone release alone. She'd thought herself above this unconscious reversion to her caveman ancestors; but, to her horror, her primal and base inner self was checking Ben Capriati out as a potential provider.

She shook herself, like a dog shaking water off its fur. No need to make a big deal of this! It was a scientific glitch: a simple case of recessive genetic memory dominating her better self. It had nothing to do with—couldn't be—*chemistry.*

Physical attraction to an underdressed, seemingly unintelligent biker who did nothing but laugh at her, when she already had a reasoned, intellectual man all her own? Ugh. It couldn't be!

It's possibly more to do with the fact that you've been all but invisible to Hugh for the past year or two, the imp whispered from the back stalls of her mind.

She tossed her head, unaware that her hair fell from its bun again, spilling her despised curls around her face. "I suppose you think you're funny. People who spend their lives contributing to the human race are something to mock. I feel sorry for you."

"If it makes you feel better," he replied with unimpaired cheerfulness. "I was about to go for a swim. Want to jump in with me, Lucy?" His eyes gleamed in wicked fun. "Swimsuit optional."

"Oh—" she gasped, trying to keep the indignation, but a sudden rush of pleasure—*someone outside my head called me Lucy!*—left her in a crazy tangle of emotions. "How could you think I'd—" She slammed her mouth shut and turned to stare at the bright, sunshiny day through the window in the open plan timber kitchen. "No. I won't swim. Thank you."

He sighed. "I was afraid of that. I'll have a shower then."

She frowned. "Why not have a swim?"

"I wasn't born yesterday. You lock me out and your four and a half tenths turns to nine…and breaking windows isn't my speed."

"I wouldn't do that. I wouldn't dream of it!" she gasped.

"Sure you wouldn't," he agreed, looking her over with open cynicism. "You look like a meek little bookworm, not a crazy home invader who'd push your way into my house or sue a kids' charity. I seem to be a bad judge of character where you're concerned. I'm not taking chances. I'm not losing my winnings that easy."

"I wouldn't sue a charity! It was a ruse to—" She sputtered to a stop, tangled inside a guilty half conviction that she might have done just that, until with a few words he'd shown her how low, how immoral that would be. "I have the right to—"

The roaring of a car motor snapped her out of her garbled outrage. "Mr. Hill—?" She bolted for the door. "I—he's gone!"

"It appears he got out while the going was good." The amused voice came from behind her, a rich, sexy baritone. "Can't say I blame him. Do you always half finish your sentences? And I wouldn't advise stepping through the door like that. Too easy for me to lock it in your face, Miss Four-and-a-half-points."

She jumped back inside the door, and fell right against him.

Oh, *help*. This primitive reaction must be more ingrained in her genetics than she'd feared. The scent of maleness and husky sweat filled her senses; the rocklike muscles holding her up seemed to force her most yielding feminine softness to come out of hiding. And looking up into those dark, laughing eyes made her pulse pound—storm, crash, hammer….

Surely she was further up the evolutionary scale than this! Such a typical female response to a handsome man was so unlike her. *I used to love this with Hugh. Hugging him after a run or a game, feeling so feminine.*

Yeah—how many years has it been since you got one of those hugs? The imp inside her muttered. *Two, three?*

"Could—could you move back, please?" she asked, but the cool dignity she'd hoped for came out as rushed breathlessness. She closed her eyes. Oh, no—what if he thought this coded genetic response was something more than a proven scientific fact? What if—what if he—and what if she—?

He stepped back.

The delicious chill in her spine died. He didn't even *try* to make a pass at her. No man ever found her irresistible. Especially not rugged, sexy cavemen like Ben Capriati.

She peeped up at him. He was grinning, as if he knew about what Hugh called her "Lucy kick": that hiding beneath her nonsense scientific facade lay a B-grade Hollywood fantasy life. Dreaming of a hero, a handsome, swashbuckling pirate to rescue her from her empty, boring life, and always being so alone…

Lifting her chin, she walked past him to the kitchen. After opening and shutting cupboards, she frowned. Most of them were empty, or held only crockery. "Where do you keep the coffee?"

Silence.

When she turned he was standing behind her, biting his lip. "What? It's not a hard question, is it?" The fridge told th same story: aside from jugs of water and juice, and som cans of beer, it was empty. "You don't have any food at all!"

"I know." He grimaced. "Well, you see, I—"

"You don't drink coffee?"

"Sure. I—"

"You ran out of everything at once?"

Ben shook his head. "No. I never had any food. I—"

"Did you just move in, and haven't had time to shop yet?

He pulled up a high-backed stool from the breakfast bench sitting backward on it. "I've been here a week."

"Then why don't you have food? Where are you eating?

Cupping his chin on propped elbows on the bench, h winked at her. "Where do you think? This is the Gold Coas Lucy. Fun in the sun, seductive pulse of the night. I eat out, drink out."

Unable to comprehend it, she blinked. "Even at *breakfast?*

"Yup." Straddling the stool, wearing only those skimp shorts and that lazy grin, he looked like a model in GQ. "Don' sound so scandalized. Think about it. Sitting at an open-ai café across from the sexiest beach on the planet. Coffee an croissants in the sun, watching the world stroll by."

His voice was warm, caressing. A vision blossomed in he mind: sitting at an open-air café with fresh croissants and caff latte, and every woman who passed them gazing wistfully wishing she was the woman with Ben….

No! The man is Hugh, and we're on our honeymoon, afte our wedding, her mind yelled at that rebellious imp. *Well, afte the experiment's over. Stop envisioning yourself with this man*

This was a ridiculous momentary confusion, all the faul of her thesis and bad genetics. All she wanted was to marr

Hugh, but a silly female in her ancestry had passed on a weakness for strong, muscled outdoor men like Ben Capriati, with a crooked grin, and twinkling dark eyes that made her insides slowly melt.

Did Hugh ever make you melt, or was it just gaining the approval of Mother and Father that mattered so much?

No! This thing she felt for Ben Capriati was passing, only physical. She'd stay here, win her prizes and sell them to pay for the wedding and fund Hugh's research. And if she had to cohabit with a rough, sexy Mediterranean Adonis—platonically, of course!—until she was declared the winner, so be it.

She was a woman of science. She had self-control. She could resist temptation—and within a week, she'd have everything she'd ever dreamed of.

She sighed and leaned on the cool fridge, feeling the world tilt back on its proper axis.

"You look like you've got the weight of the world on your shoulders," he said, watching her with curious gentleness.

"Lack of caffeine," she murmured, locked in visions of bridal splendour. "I slept in the car last night."

Even lost in glorious daydreams of tulle and lace and white carriages, she could hear a frown of concern in his voice. "Why didn't you get a room? There's hundreds of 'em to spare before summer. High-school graduation isn't for three weeks."

She snapped to attention, frowning. "What business is that of yours, Mr. Capriati?"

"Ben."

Hmm. Nice, masculine name. "Okay," she murmured, with only a little reluctance. "Mind your own business, Ben."

His eyebrow lifted. "Did you at least have breakfast?"

"I won't even dignify that with an answer." Yet, as if in rebellion with her pride, her stomach growled. Loudly.

He laughed and hauled himself off the stool, his six-pack and shoulder muscles rippling with the movement. "No wonder you're cranky. Come on, let's eat. We'll take the convertible. You might as well enjoy our disputed prizes while you can. Give me a couple of minutes to shower."

He bounded up the stairs two and three at a time. She gulped, watching him from behind...*okay, so I'm watching his behind—so what? It's a coded feminine reaction.* And those shorts made him look so strong and athletic, so perfectly proportioned—

"So is Hugh—he's in perfect shape," she muttered.

You just haven't seen him in anything but his lab coat for a really long time.

She wheeled away to look out the window. This situation was out of control already. What could she do?

Call Hugh. Yes! She needed his calm voice, his practical reassurance to help her get past this stupid internal glitch, telling her against all logic that Ben Capriati was...was...

Highly attractive? Sexy? Downright gorgeous?

No! I'm just out of my element. I'm taking in new experiences—and of course a man like Ben is attractive to all women.

Say it, Lucy, the imaginary imp, her only friend in her isolated world as a child, urged her on. *You've never had time off before, never been off the leash. You've never even been able to talk without Mother and Father and Hugh telling you that what you want and say and think is wrong—and you're already having the time of your life!*

And the worst part of it was, she didn't even feel guilty—and she didn't *want* to call Hugh, either.

The thunder of feet thumping down the stairs halted her in her tracks; her hand froze over the phone. Either she'd been lost in thought for ages, or Ben took the world's fastest shower. He was back, wearing surf shorts, a T-shirt and slip-on shoes, his hair dripping wet. Even in such an innocuous

outfit he looked dark, dangerous and blatantly masculine—
like a dreaming pirate.

How was she going to spend days and nights in the company of this man, without succumbing to the temptation of—

He grabbed her hand. "So let's do it."

She looked down at her hand nestled in his, then up to his
face, to the eyes full of bedroom twinkle and a chin of five
o'clock shadow even before lunch. Her heart pounding beneath her ribs, she managed to stutter, "D-do—do it?"

"Yeah. You're hungry. I'm hungry. You need caffeine. Let's
sit in the sun and watch the world walk past."

"I—but—" She blinked to reorient herself. Right. Kitchen.
House. Going out for coffee and food. "What's the purpose
of this excursion? We could buy groceries and stock the house
to cook—"

"The purpose, Lucy, is to have fun. F.U.N. Ever hear of it?"

She pulled her hand out of his, stung by the unspoken ac-
cusation. "Don't you work?"

"Not in November—it's fun-and-games month," he shot
back, laughing. "We both want to eat, so we might as well im-
prove our tans and your temper while we do it. C'mon, Lucy,
we're holed up together, so why not relax? This is the Gold
Coast. The laid-back and kick-off-your-shoes vacation capi-
tal of Australia. Enjoy it. Soak it in."

She hesitated. "Well, I suppose, since we've been forced
to stay together—"

"—we might as well enjoy ourselves while we suspect
each other of felonious activities," he finished cheerfully.

A sidelong glance. "I want a set of keys to the house."

He leaned over to the wooden rack at the side of the fridge,
and handed her a set of keys. "Satisfied?"

"Not until I try them out." Thrusting out her chin, she dared
him. "You go through the door first."

"Uh-uh. No way." He grabbed both her hands, linking his fingers through hers. "Consider us superglued and handcuffed. What we do, we do together until this situation's untangled."

She eyed the doorway, thinking of the implications of his words with a half-guilty thrill. "We won't fit," she argued, her mind filled with delicious, forbidden visions.

He looked her over. "You're a bitty thing. A tight squeeze, but we'll just make it, in my professional opinion."

"Professional what?"

"Professional door-squeezer," he returned promptly—too promptly? Her eyes narrowed, staring at him. Was he hiding something inside the words? "C'mon, Lucy, superglued and handcuffed—or will you trust me not to lock the door in your face after you go first? Me being the gentleman I am and all."

"I—I don't know if I should—"

As if he knew all her hidden fears, he leaned close and whispered, "A whole new world awaits, Lucy Miles, scientific librarian. All you have to do is walk through that door."

A new world. Oh, he was more right than he knew, and the idea scared her more than she'd admit. But she'd stepped outside her cloistered world last night, the door already breached. There was no turning back now. Taking a deep breath she charged to the door and opened it with a defiant toss of her head, like a warrior going into the Crusades. "Well, let's do it."

Those expressive dark eyes filled with laughter as he turned sideways, grabbing her other hand again. "Crabs."

She gasped. "What?"

He pulled her against him. "Crab-walking's the only way we'll get out of here under our superglued and handcuffed, chained-to-each-other policy. Let's go."

Uh-oh. Just as well he was holding her up, for her stupid genetic code chose that precise moment to act out again. So a woman's knees could turn weak at the touch of a man's body. At the feel of skin against skin, male against female, muscled strength against tender femininity...

What am I thinking? Science, wedding, Hugh—SCIENCE!

Yes, she could focus...just as soon as she could stop *feeling* his strong chest and taut stomach muscles against her as they shuffled sideways together. When the strange sweetness of his muscled arm around her waist wore off. And when that fresh male scent he wore stopped making her head spin so deliciously...

Ben had the door shut before she realized they were outside. "Welcome back to the outside world. Want to test out your keys?"

Oops, she was still walking sideways—and clinging to him. "Oh. Yes, of course."

The keys worked just fine. Deflated, she turned back to him, but couldn't look up. "Thank you," she mumbled.

"For what?"

"For not cheating." She gave a little, embarrassed shrug.

"I'm not that much of a Neanderthal, Lucy, I promise."

She looked up, seeing no hint of laughter in his eyes. He looked awkward, even hurt. She bit her lip. "I'm sorry, Ben."

"You have an amazing voice." He smiled then, a personal, spine-tingling look. "All breathy and voluptuous. Little girlish, yet all woman. You know, like the way Marilyn Monroe sang 'Happy Birthday' to JFK."

Oh, yes, she knew...the dress, the woman, the powerful male...

"I suspect untold depths live and pulse beneath that cardigan of yours," Ben said softly. "What's going on in your mind to put such a dazed, sexy look on your face?"

The bubble burst. "I'm not sexy!"

"You know, an hour ago, I'd have agreed with you. I thought you were a drudge at first." He shook his head, and that rebel lock of hair fell back over his forehead. "But you've changed so many times in the past hour, I can't wait to see what comes next. I suspect you're a lady of mercurial depths beneath your prosaic exterior, Lucy Miles. I'd love to see you lose the cardigan."

"No!" she gasped, pulling it tighter around her.

"And let your hair down, spilling all over your shoulders," continued the sinuous voice of temptation in her ear.

"Never!"

"And barefoot, running free in the wind and sun, that soft, creamy skin of yours all flushed and hot…"

Hmm…

Stop it!

She kept a close hold of her sweater, glaring at him. "Well, you won't, and that's all. Ben—Mr. Capriati—I'm engaged, and I won't take off my cardigan for any man but Hugh!"

To her dismay, he burst out laughing.

"What?" she demanded, exasperated. Why did he keep laughing at her when no one else ever thought she was funny?

He fell against the wall, in gasping chuckles. "Now I see your problem—you were born in the wrong century. You won't *take off your cardigan for me?*" He doubled right over.

Tears sprang to her eyes. "That was unkind of you to say," she whispered. "And—and you're wrong. Mother and Father and Hugh are all wrong. I am not a genetic throwback. I am not a poor, submissive little woman who's only good for supporting things more important than me! I'm a human being, and you will treat me with basic respect, d-do you understand?" She scrubbed at her eyes.

He looked at her for a long moment, with a quiet soberness in his handsome face. "I didn't mean it. I was jerking your chain. Teasing is my worst habit, according to my family. I'm sorry." He spoke with the same awkward sincerity

e'd used over the keys. "C'mon, let's go. I won't laugh at you
ny more. Scout's honor."

"Were you ever a Scout?" she asked doubtfully.

He grinned then. "Suspicious woman. You wound me,
ucy-babe. Just coffee, croissants and pleasant conversation,
swear."

She resisted the urge to smile, but it was oh, so hard. "I
on't trust you an inch." Her stomach rumbled again in ag-
ressive protest, and they both laughed. "Well, all right, but
m only coming for the food. And *don't call me babe!*"

Chapter Three

She'd never been in a convertible before…

So seductive. With the top down, they roared through th[e]
beachside city. The warm wind blew through her hair, th[e]
spring sun touched her skin, and a dark, dangerous man s[at]
beside her, who even made changing gears a sensual care[ss]
of the stick. A capable male as well as physically attractive.

Stop thinking about it!

She couldn't help it. Surfer's Paradise was known as th[e]
Sin City of Queensland. Hot temptation beckoned ever[y]
where; seduction breathed in every pore. It had a life all i[ts]
own, pulsing from a twenty-mile strip of creamy-whi[te]
sand—the soft rhythmic throb of spilling waves, its glitterin[g]
duty-free stores and luxury hotels. Cosmopolitan eateries an[d]
open-air markets, pubs, casinos and nightclubs lined ever[y]
corner.

I can respect you, Abigail. You're so high-minded, abo[ve]
wanting all the flashy, superficial things other women crav[e]

Bad girl. Bad girl, the imp whispered. *And oh, aren't we njoying it for once...*

Then Ben roared into a parking space on the strip in front f all the unbroken sand and surf. "Not bad, eh? Doesn't my weet Jessica purr like a kitten? And you've got to admit the cenery's not half-bad." His voice caressed her, wafting over er heated skin like a lover's touch. "No lab test can repro-luce it, no photo lab can airbrush it. Heat and sand and the oolness of the waves, a brilliantine sky you could almost walk into. The sexiest strip of land on earth. Like a siren song or the senses."

Lucy turned to look at him in despair. What was this man, ate's punishment for her secret life? "Jessica?" she croaked.

"Hmm." Ben's hand glided in slow appreciation along the lash. "My Jessica. She reminds me of an old flame of mine. .ong and sleek and fast, oozing sensuality."

She shook her head to clear the graphic image. "Listen to ourself. You're talking about a car, Ben. A car! Honestly, lon't you think of anything but sex?"

He grinned. "Not when you rise to the bait every time. You're like a wriggling fish on a hook. I can't resist."

"Does Jessica exist?" she demanded.

He gave her a rueful grin. "I wasn't laughing at you this ime—just teasing you a bit." He touched her face, smiling whimsically. "You look so adorable when you gape at me. Or when you blush. Especially when you blush."

She bit her lip, feeling the tide of color fill her cheek. Every time she thought she had him pegged, he said things hat were so completely *enchanting*....

"Yeah, that's the one. It's cute, sweet—and so sexy."

The violin symphony in her head came to a screeching alt. "I'm engaged. You shouldn't be saying things like that o me!"

He shrugged, keeping an obvious distance. "It's just harmless fun, Lucy. Talking doesn't have to become doing." He gave her a genuinely puzzled look. "Haven't you ever flirted before—just for fun? I'm not going to proposition you."

"I have more important things to do with my life." Heat scalded her face now. *Had* she ever flirted with a man? Did she know how? "This is a ridiculous conversation." She leaped out of the car and stalked ahead of him to the main boulevard.

Within seconds he'd caught up with her, and led her to an outdoor restaurant in the sunshine, across from the beach. "You would frequent a café that becomes a bar at night," she muttered.

"You really need to lighten up, Lucy." He seated her at a table, sat down opposite her and waved a hand over the glorious vista. "Look at it. Soak it in. Warm sun, white sand, the sound and scent of surf, the beautiful people strolling by."

"With nothing better to do than stroll," she remarked, trying to ignore those seductive sights and scents. "Don't they work?"

The waitress arrived, and they gave their orders; then Ben leaned back in his chair, face tilted up to the warm, cloudless sky. "Should people spend all their time working?"

"Why not? Man is a working animal, and—"

"Are you talking about yourself, or your fiancé?" She felt herself crimson with guilt and confusion. The incredulity was plain in his voice as he asked, "You mean your fiancé doesn't even take days off to spend time with you?"

She bit her lip. *He's a stranger. He can't make you cry.* "He's a dedicated scientist, helping people in need. And at least he works, not like some people."

He leaned back in his chair, pushing his sunglasses farther up his nose. "You know, that's a bad habit of yours. We met less than two hours ago, yet you think you've got me all figured out. What if you're wrong?"

"Maybe I did jump to conclusions—but you did, too, in judging Hugh without even having met him," she pointed out.

He bit his lip; a quirky, rueful grin emerged. "Touché, my friend. Good call. So I did. Very immature of me."

"You're right, I shouldn't have said it—but look at you." A hand swept over him. "You're here doing nothing at all. You win those wonderful prizes, and use them to foster a sedentary lifestyle instead of getting a decent trade—"

Ben's mouth quivered with the need to laugh. Man, she was cute when she was off on one of her tangents and so totally different from any other woman who saw him as *Ben, the doctor,* with all the potential for a comfortable lifestyle it implied, that he couldn't resist keeping up the beach-bum image. He'd finally met one young, unmarried woman who didn't see him as a potential source of future funds, and somehow it charmed him. "I'm thirty-one, Lucy. Do you think anyone's going to take me on as their apprentice now?"

Their orders came, and the glorious scent of warm caffe latte and fresh, hot croissants assailed her roiling stomach. She snatched up a croissant and buttered it, spreading thick jam over it, and gulped down the first mouthful with an ecstatic sigh. "Maybe not—but any college would take you as a student," she mumbled, her mouth full. "You could have a decent job—maybe with computers—within months. It could change your life!"

"Ick. Can't imagine sitting on my butt at a computer all my life." Ben buttered his croissant as she wolfed hers down with an ecstasy so strong she couldn't contain it. "And I've already done the university-college trip. I don't plan on repeating it anytime soon." He grinned and winked at her.

Her tirade halted abruptly. Oh, why did he have to smile like that? He made it a species all its own: warm, intimate, as if she was the only woman in the world…. She gulped down coffee, scorching her mouth. "You've been to university?"

He lifted the shades, highlighting the thick black lashes fringing his eyes: dark, exotic, with the luscious, inherent sensuality of a Mediterranean background. She'd always had a guilty passion for Italian men. "Ask nicely, Lucy, and you shall receive." When she frowned, confused, he said softly, "Say my name in the sexy voice of yours, and I'm putty in your hands."

She struggled, torn between indignation and temptation, but it seemed she'd left her self-control behind in Sydney, and she couldn't resist. "Have you been to university—Ben?"

"Aaah, that's the one." He leaned back in his chair, folding his hands behind his head. "I've been to university. I endured years of it, so I'll never go back, whether it makes me a dropout or not."

She wanted to condemn him for his lack of staying power, but she was led on by a raging curiosity to know more about the sort of man who'd not only always been off-limits, but was also her secret fantasy. A dark, dangerous bad boy. "And you're Italian?"

"My dad is—hence the name Capriati. He was born to a pair of Bronx-born Sicilian-Americans who moved to Sydney in the early fifties, when he was seventeen."

She blinked at the sudden overload of information. "Your father's American?"

"With a strange half Bronx, half Australian accent to boot." He laughed. "My mother's Irish-Australian, and Papa's family, proud of their Sicilian heritage, have barely forgiven her for the crime—not to mention that they met only two days before his wedding to a nice Italian girl." An inscrutable look passed over his face. "Mama and Papa got married four months later."

Obviously, that was a subject to leave alone. "I'm Irish, too—well, my grandparents were, on both parents' sides," she said, smiling. "Do the family punish you for being Australian?"

"I was always bigger than them, so they didn't get too nasty." He winked again. "Now it's my turn. Do you have brothers or sisters?"

She shook her head. "My parents had me when they were in their early forties. I was—unplanned."

"But not unwelcome?"

She gulped more coffee. She'd been having fun; the last thing she wanted to do right now was to think about her life. Her father and mother were always so dedicated to science, her birth and upbringing having been somewhat of an afterthought for them both. Her grandparents had died before she'd been born, and with no other relatives in the country, she'd been brought up in special preschools and advanced learning centres aimed at developing her potential. In all her life, she'd rarely spent time with her parents except in the car, and at dinner. *Shush, Abigail, no talking at the table. Your father's trying to think, and I have papers to mark.* "No," she answered, her voice scratchy. "Not unwelcome."

"What made you become a science librarian? You said your parents were scientists. Was it genetic, or exposure?"

She shrugged. "I always loved books. I spent a lot of time in the university library after school." *Go read a book, Abigail. We're busy.* "To become a librarian seemed a natural progression. Do you have brothers or sisters?" she asked, to turn the subject.

"Three younger brothers, Joe, Marco and Jack, and just one sister, Sofie—and believe me, she's enough. She more than outyells all four of us guys." He mock-grimaced. "She never shuts up. I put a padlock on my door just for some peace when I lived at home."

"You don't know how lucky you are." As a little girl, she'd been scared sometimes that the silence would drive her mad. Oh, how she'd wished for a big, noisy family to love. "Don't take your family for granted."

He grinned. "I wouldn't dare. Now let's cheer up. We're out in the sunshine, by the beach—"

She sighed and put her mug down with a rattle. "Ben…"

"Hey, come on, Lucy, give it a rest. A week off won't destroy the world." He shook his head. "Do you know what a sexy voice you have, by the way? It's like a fantasy come to life—"

"You have fantasies, too?" With a wide-open grin of joy she pounced on him. "I've always had—"

"Aha!" He grinned at her as she stuffed her runaway mouth with croissant. "I knew there were untold depths to plumb beneath that prim, sterile facade of yours, Abigail Lucinda Miles."

The croissant nearly choked her. "Sterile. *Sterile!*" she gasped, in an outrage totally disproportionate to the word.

"Yeah. Like a lab bench. Germfree. Without spot from the world." Flipping his shades up to rest on his hair, he watched her in amusement, leaning right back until the chair seemed ready to crash on the pavement. "But I suspect the volcano of repressed human emotion is about to erupt all over me."

"W-well, it's your fault," she hiccupped, feeling too indignant to care how she spoke to him. "You called me *sterile*—"

"I beg your pardon, Ms. Miles. Obviously I was wrong." He sipped his coffee, still watching her in lazy interest. "So, was the *S* word the catalyst for this volatile chemical reaction in your emotive recesses to allow you to admit to a fantasy life, or was I somehow involved?"

"The *s* word," she returned far too quickly.

"Uh-uh, Lucy. You're fibbing. The original sexy dreamer's look was on your face long before I said the dreaded *s* word. Well, what do you know." His grin grew wide. "A guy like me—the kind you despise—is a catalyst for your feminine fantasies."

Hating that he'd plumbed the truth inside her silly, unscientific soul, she mumbled, "It's not you. It's the crazy things you say! All that talk of beaches and sun and singing to the president—"

"You like that one?" His voice was soft, enticing. "We could act it out if you want. I'd love to play president to that gorgeous Marilyn voice of yours."

Don't go there! But the vision flashed into her mind: plain, uninteresting Abigail Lucinda Miles in a shimmering white gown, singing to this gorgeous caveman—her every breathy word filled with sensual promise....

A caress on her palm, warm and tender as the touch of a wafting breeze. "Tell me your dreams and fantasies, Lucy, and I could help make them come true."

Lost, helpless, she gazed at him. The man she'd written off as an ignorant caveman understood her better than her own family; he knew more about her in four hours than the man she'd been in love with for six years. For the first time in twenty-eight years she had a kindred spirit—a man who slotted right into those fantasies as if he'd always lived there. If she wanted to play...

Abigail, dear, do try not to be so selfish. Hugh's work helps humanity.

She bit her lip, frowned, closed her eyes and blurted it out. "No, I don't *want*. I don't want anything from you but my prizes." She stuffed the croissant in her mouth, jumped to her feet and took off running for the car.

Ben watched her bolt, and sighed. "You and your big mouth, Capriati," he grumbled. "You should have known it was too early to put the plan in action." He stalked inside, dumped some money on the counter and took off after her.

Lucy ran as fast as she could, but he caught up to her a minute later. "Lucy, wait."

"Go away!" She kept stalking down the hot pavement, past

sunshine-soaked beach apartment buildings and waving palms and tropical gardens toward the car.

He strode around her, blocking her flight right in a patch of melting, ocean-scented sunlight. He took her jaw in his hand, gently making her look at him. "I was just teasing. And even if I wasn't, it's nothing to be ashamed of. Everyone has their little dreams, even the scientific giants. Think of them— Einstein, Bell, Franklin, the Curies, Galileo. Without their dreams, the world would be a poorer place."

Lucy peeped up at him, blinking, as dazed as if she stood on shifting ground. "N-no. That's not right. Hugh doesn't dream."

"Sure he does." The hand touching her chin moved a fraction, not enough to be called a caress. "What does he do in his line? Treat people, or is he into the research side of things?"

"R-research," she replied, barely realizing she was purring.

"So he's looking to find some new cure, something no one else has found. That's his dream."

"That's not his dream, it's his *goal*. It's vital to have goals. My dreams are nothing life changing. They're just…silly."

"That's what they thought about Ben Franklin. People said Einstein was crazy." Gentle hands fell on her wrists, pushing her sleeves up her arms. The cool sea breeze caressed her heated flesh, and she sighed in unconscious relief. She was so hot…. "Your dreams may not save the world, but if they make you happy, and they don't hurt anyone, why not indulge a little?"

"I—I can't…." She licked her upper lip, scared, fascinated and so tempted….

Are you ready for this? If you go forward, you can never go back and when this time's over with Ben, you'll be all alone.

She jerked out from under his mesmerizing touch. "N-no.

No! You're wrong. Self-discipline and hard work is the key to true happiness, fulfillment and career achievement!"

"Fulfillment and career achievement. You sound like a parrot," he muttered in disgust. "Who taught you that rubbish?"

She frowned and looked away. "I can think for myself," she said quietly. "And even if it were from my parents or fiancé, it's not your place to call it rubbish. I don't belittle your family or beliefs."

"You're right. I'm sorry." He threw up his hands. "And I know the basic premise of what you said is right. There are millions of wonderful people who spend their lives caring for others or to make medical or scientific breakthroughs, and that's great. But they want to do that. If they choose it—if it gives them pleasure, and helps others—well, good for them. But if you fulfill your harmless dreams for a few days, and make yourself happy—why deny yourself of that? What good does that do for you, your family or the world?"

She almost grabbed the tree for balance as the world rocked beneath her. Was—was Ben right? Hugh and her parents *were* happy, doing what they wanted with their lives—but was she? "But they're noble, and I'm so banal." Her head drooped in shame. "Hugh and my father want to save future generations from deadly diseases…my mother wants to educate people, and my dreams are to water-ski and swim with dolphins!"

"Hey, nice call. I'd love to try it—and it's doable. We'll hire the gear and a driver, and take a day trip out to South Stradbroke Island." He smiled at her. "Think of it, Lucy. Serene warm ocean, the sensation of flying through the air and water at once. Swimming with the loveliest of God's creatures."

Stamping her foot in frustration, she whacked the pavement. "Ow! No, you don't understand! Hugh wants to change the DNA strand that causes Down's syndrome or spina bifida, and all I want to do is kiss a dark stranger on a crowded dance floor!"

Ben shrugged. "Why not? I'm sure the stranger won't object, especially if you got that curvy body into a little black dress and let your hair down, showing off your gorgeous face."

"I'm not curvy, I'm not gorgeous and I'm engaged, that's why not!" she wailed. "I'm marrying my perfect man in three months." *If you can get him to remember it, Abigail.* "My wedding's all planned!"

"Well, there's nothing to stop you, if you get help now. And, lucky for you, help exists." He smiled again, and something inside flipped right over itself. "Here I am, willing, able and here for a week's worth of unfulfilled dreams. I can help you get all this out of your system, tax free. If it will make you feel better, we can think of this as a project. Like a scientific experiment." He took a step closer.

She stared at him, eyebrows knit in perplexity. "Experiment?"

"Yup." He reached out, touching her arms.

Lost in thought, scared and exhilarated and doubtful all at once, she didn't notice the touch on a conscious level. "How?"

He touched her nose with a finger. "You're getting pink. We'd better get you out of the sun. Lucy, have you ever wondered what would happen if your fantasies became a reality?"

"Yes—no!"

"Take a minute now. Think about it." How could his touch be soothing and arousing at the same time? As gentle as a brother, yet as tempting as honeyed sin? "Think about your sweet, harmless dreams coming true. I'm talking in a purely scientific way."

Her head snapped up. He had her full attention now. "How can fulfilling my fantasies be scientific?" she asked breathlessly.

"Okay. What possibilities are there? Analyze it, Lucy."

Analyze...analyze. Right. I can do that. Ben's fingers are walking up my arms. Those big, dark hands of his are as soft as butterfly wings, and it's making me tingle in the strangest places. I feel all warm and flushed and—and delicious...

"Lucy, are you analyzing?"

"Mmm," she sighed, wrapped in her gorgeous dreamland.

"I can see you are. You look so hot," he murmured. "Don't you think you'd be more comfortable with that cardigan off—and maybe your shoes, too?"

"Hmm. Cardigan off…yes. What?" She glared at him, more furious with herself than him. Ben Capriati was a stranger, a man totally unknown to her yesterday. How could he have put himself into the center of her fantasy world in just over three hours?

No…not the dreams about my lovely wedding. They always have Hugh at the end of the aisle!

Comforted and emboldened by the realization, yet too curious to let the subject go, she faced him in would-be cool challenge. "Just give me your version of the so-called scientific analysis."

Ben sighed. "Okay. The way I see it, there are two major possibilities in this analysis. One, the worst-case scenario—you become addicted to having fantasy fulfillment, wanting more and more of it. You'd have to take a chance with that. But to my mind, the second possibility is stronger—maybe as each of your fantasies come to life, you put it behind you forever. Over. *Fini.* Kaput. And then you're free as a bird—free to return to your pristine world and become Mrs. Dr. What's-his-name."

Glory, glory hallelujah! If he'd pushed a button inside her that read "Abandon conscience, all ye who enter here," he couldn't have grabbed her runaway mind more effectively. To make these crazy thoughts and half hopes disappear forever…by acting on them, no less. It was a brilliant idea!

She gazed up into those dark eyes, framed by a rebel midnight mane, and was lost. "Do—do you think?" she whispered, with no breath left to speak.

He looked down at her, his expression hard to define—but her lifelong gift for human analysis had taken wings with his magical words. "I think. I really think."

Just as well he was, because her brain was mush. If Ben was willing to help her shed her unwanted double life…"And you don't mind helping me?"

He laughed, looking more raffish than ever. "I'd be proud to be of assistance to you, ma'am. All in the cause of scientific interest, naturally."

"You'd just be a—a catalyst."

He lifted his hands in mock innocence. "A catalyst only."

She peeped up at him. "I can ask anything?"

"So long as there's no weddings or questions on fathering your future heirs, I'm game. Marriage and babies and me—well, they just aren't compatible at this point in the game."

"Weddings and babies, with *you?*" She waved that away. "Of course not. Why would I want you for that, when I have Hugh?"

"I've never met the guy, but already I can see why you'd prefer him to me," he replied dryly.

She nodded, lost in her thoughts. "Of course. Anyone would. Sure you've got the looks, the daring and sense of adventure—but I want a man I can respect. Hugh's stable. He's brilliant. He wants to save lives. He looks to the future—everything's planned. Anyone can see you don't think a minute ahead."

"Uh, right. I'm obviously the original brainless beach bum."

Again she nodded, too lost in thought to truly register the strange note in Ben's voice. "He never has to know about this."

"I'll never tell him. Wild horses, etc." He took her hand and solemnly crossed his heart with it…right over that muscled chest, and springing dark hair.

Her legs turned to rubber.

Soft padding pushed behind her weakened knees—and it

was only then she realized he'd led her back to the car. She snuggled into the loving embrace of plush leather with a deep sigh. "And surely it would be a better start for our marriage if I were more *settled*. Wanting my future without doubt or fear."

"Sure."

Suspicious of all this agreement, she looked at him, seated on the other side of her. "I'll be back in Sydney in a few days, and nobody will be any the wiser. Right?" she demanded.

"Right. They'll have to torture me to get the information." He started the engine of the convertible.

Her convertible!

"With my prizes to fund my wedding, and Hugh's experiment," she reminded him sharply.

He grinned at her. "We're into fantasies here. I'll indulge this one for now."

The bubble burst. "Why? Why are you being so nice to me? Why are you trying to help me with this? What's in it for you?"

"Such a suspicious woman." He patted her hand. "I'm just helping a fellow creature in distress."

"You don't seem the type to act from the generosity of your heart—and I'm not in distress," she snapped.

He turned to her, with a strange, serious look. "Are you sure you're not, Lucy?"

Caught in the honesty of those Mediterranean eyes, unable to even speak in bravado, she floundered in silence.

All her life, she'd been trained that it was fine and noble to sacrifice her life and wants for science, and the greater good of humanity. And until yesterday—today—she'd believed it. Now her world was turning upside down. She didn't know what she thought or believed anymore, except for one thing. She was tired of giving up everything for science!

As if he understood her dilemma, he drove out into traffic.

"If a few dreams help you feel happier about life while you're waiting for your wedding, where's the harm?"

Put like that, she suddenly was unable to find any harm…and breathless anticipation filled her. Oh, to have just one or two dreams come true… "Okay, I'll agree, so long as you stop touching me all the time. Why *do* you do that?"

He lifted his hands from the wheel for a moment and looked at them, as if he wanted to know the answer, too. Then he showed one palm to her in mock surrender. "Don't take it personally. I'm from a tactile family."

"Well, I'm not, so I'd prefer it if you didn't, okay?" She shook her hair, tumbling around in the breeze, pins and bands long since left behind. "Why would a man who didn't know me four hours ago want to make my fantasies come true? Why do you care if I live my life in a *sterile* lab? Why do you care if I never water-ski, swim with dolphins—" she blushed "—or any of the other things I should never have told you about?"

"All right. You want the truth?" He sighed, shifting gears. The sensual gesture, the scent of leather rising from the seats, the sweet springtime wind and sun drew her into a languid spell. "It's easy to see how unhappy you are. You're just dying to break the mold, to escape the rut you're in, but you're too scared to come out of the closet without a little help."

She gaped at him, lost again. Was she—her unhappiness— so transparent? And if it was, why didn't the people who were closest to her, ever seem to notice what a stranger had seen in a few hours? "W-what help?"

He shrugged. "Nothing illegal, Lucy. I just wanted to give you some fun for a few days. I can't stand to see a girl as full of life as you are not even knowing what it means to enjoy your-self. You're so unhappy you don't know what happiness is."

She didn't know what to say to that. Dreaming, planning

or happiness as something so intangible, she'd never found
. She was always thinking, *I'll be happy when*—when she
ound a man to love, when she had her perfect wed-
ing…when she had her parents' approval for once.

He glanced at her for a moment and sighed—and if her face
ooked half as frozen as she felt right now, she could under-
tand why. "It's true, Lucy. You seem to think going out to eat
s a sin, you drive a car that should be condemned and wear
lothes that hide what a total babe you are. I want to see you
augh and play and have fun. I want to see you laughing and
oyous and *happy*." He tipped up her sagging jaw with that
heeky grin that made her bones give that funny warm shiver.
Abigail Lucinda Miles, you need a physical and emotional
nakeover—and I'm just the guy to do it for you."

Chapter Four

Watching the waves crash on the vista of silver-bright beach behind her, Ben held his breath for her reaction—and, in h peripheral vision, he saw Lucy's jaw drop. "Y-you w-what?

Unable to look at her he shrugged. "It's no biggie, Lucy. want to do a makeover on you. I want you to find out wh you are, to get new clothes, to eat out, drink out and just hav irresponsible fun for a week." He held his breath, waiting f her to laugh at him, turn away in embarrassment, show hie den interest—

But the last thing he expected was fury: heated, incred lous outrage. "What are you, a frustrated ten-year-old? I'm n a human Barbie doll or a chimp in a cage to experiment on

"No, you're not," he agreed gently, trying to look in h eyes, but she'd half averted her flushed face. "But what a you, Lucy Miles? *Who* are you? Why do your family call yo Abigail when I assume you've told them you don't like i Why doesn't your fiancé ever take time off to be with yo

Why do you wear secondhand clothes? Why did you sleep in the car last night?"

Her face lifted to his, and the stricken look in her eyes stabbed his heart. "I—I don't want to talk about it."

"You could have been in real danger, sleeping in the car," he pressed.

"It—it's none of your concern." The warm wind picked up her glowing curls; the sun shone on her soft, creamy skin. So lovely, and so *vulnerable...*

Ben ached for her. All his life he'd collected strays, and this adorable little waif touched his soul with her mercurial moods, her wistfulness and bravado. Someone had to make her life their concern, even if it was only for a week. Someone had to teach her to care for her needs, to find out what *she* wanted from life. "Lucy, someone could have attacked you. Carjackings happen here as well as Sydney. Women are assaulted here, too."

She gave a mirthless chuckle. "There was no danger of that, with the car I have—and this face," she said wryly.

Somehow, the ache got even worse. She didn't even know how pretty she was. "I wouldn't count on that. You intrigue me, Lucy. You have from first sight. There's so much to discover inside the package you present to the world."

"Really?" she whispered, her eyes filled with wide-eyed incredulity, as if he'd said something special and wonderful.

Oh, help. When she gave him that wistful look, out of those big Irish eyes of hers...

No way, Capriati. This is not the Curse! Your life's great as it is. Complicating it with feelings for this girl would turn you into the same kind of needing, emotional, out-of-control ness all the other Capriati men get into with the Curse. She's a sweet kid, and you feel sorry for her, that's all. Keep it cool and under control.

"Definitely. There's an indefinable magic shining from in side you. Maybe it's Lucy, the gentle dreamer, fighting to liv without Abigail's starchy, dominating factor."

She gasped, her face glowing now. "You—you like *me* You really like Lucy better?" she whispered.

Whoa—the transformation of her, from a simple affirm ing statement. Her cheeks flushed; her eyes grew brighte every moment until she glowed with joy. She was so prett and old-fashioned and lovely, like a wild rose…. "Much be ter. Who wouldn't?" *Besides, obviously, your family.* Hov these people could be so blind was beyond him. Why wouldn't like Lucy?

She sighed and shook her head, and he knew she was think ing of that family of hers. Her fiancé, too? Did he prefe starchy Abigail to the sweet dreamer Lucy?

Finally, she spoke. "Why do you care whether I'm happ or not? We only met today, and we're worlds apart. We hav absolutely nothing in common."

Yeah, she's right. She's a scientific princess, the only chil of professors. She's light-years above my two-jobs-throug college, oldest-kid-of-five backstreets life. "Does that mean w can't be friends, and have a week of harmless fun? I'm no asking for anything in return, Lucy, except that you think c me with a smile when it's over."

"Why would you want to do this for me?" She shook he head. "I don't understand."

"Why wouldn't I?" he asked, puzzled.

"Well, it's not like I'd inspire chivalry, is it? I barely inspir a memory." Her hand swept over her crumpled clothes, he mussed hair. "I'm the mousy girl guys stumble past on the way to the popular bombshells."

Oh, heck, now his heart was aching again. *Oh, Lucy—yo don't even know you're adorable….* "Hugh must have looke at you," he reminded her, when he'd conquered the primitive need to ram a fist down someone's throat.

"Yes." Her eyes grew misty. "My parents brought Hugh home to meet me. I couldn't believe it when he asked me to partner him to a function the next week. I mean, why me? He's so superior—he has a double doctorate. He's a prodigy. All the girls at the library think he's the best-looking man on campus, too. What did he see in someone like me?"

Sheesh. The guy was smart, but Lucy truly thought this guy was *superior* to her. What on earth had her parents taught her, to make her think so little of herself? "So he must have noticed you in the first place, to ask your parents if he could meet you?"

"O-oh...." She gave him a big, joyous smile. "Do—do you think? I always assumed it was the other way—that my parents talked him into meeting me. But he *did* tell me I was the most modest, sensible, level-headed woman he'd ever known...."

Ick. That was a compliment she treasured? "I'm sure he must have told you how beautiful you are, at least once."

"He will, when he sees me in my wedding dress," she said, her voice halfway between determined and wobbly.

At that, compassion swamped him. "He will. Trust me."

"Thank you, Ben." She leaned over and kissed his cheek. And so what if it heated him up more than any tongue-tangling encounters with the nightclub babes he knew? It was just a quick endorphin kick betraying him. "You can be such a nice person, when you try...."

He grinned to hide his urge to turn his face, to feel the power her full-on kiss would give. "So my mother tells me."

She smiled back in shy teasing. "I bet that's not all she says. You must have been quite a handful as a child."

"Not a time she remembers with fondness," he joked, to keep that smile lighting her piquant face. "I was hell on wheels—bike, scooter, skateboard, car, motorbike..."

"Motorbike?" The question was soft, breathless; the quaint, dreamy look was back.

"Yeah."

She peeped at him, biting her lip as if she didn't dare hope. "It—it wouldn't be a Harley, would it?"

"Sorry," he replied gruffly. "It's an Aprilia Mille R."

"Oh, Aprilias are so elegant." She closed her eyes and sighed. "Poetry in motion."

Now *that* was a shock. "You know about Aprilias?"

She nodded. "I've always loved bikes—especially the pretty ones. Harleys have the name. Ducatis have the reputation. But Aprilias are so pretty—and I hear they give a beautiful ride."

His heart turned to warm slush at her wistful tone. "Elegant and pretty. That's what I thought the first time I saw my Mille. After one ride, I had to buy her. She's at home in the garage."

"Do you think…would it be too much trouble…?"

He gave up waiting for her to ask. "You want a ride?"

Her grin grew big and brilliant as the sun bursting over the ocean. "At sunrise," she got out in a rush. "On the beach."

"Such a romantic soul," he teased gently. "How about a ride on the water's edge?" His hand waved toward the long strip of ocean by the road, past Sea World on the other side of the bay.

She pouted a little. "No ride on the beach?"

"No way. It would amount to bike abuse. If I get sand in the engine, it will leave us stranded."

"Oh, I didn't think of that. Thank you, Ben." She smiled valiantly. "I've never been on a bike before. It sounds wonderful."

His gut tightened. *Oh, Lucy, stop smiling at me like that!*

He shook himself, and started the car. "I'll do almost anything for you during the experiment, Lucy…except get sand in the engine."

"Or be the man in my wedding pictures, or father my babies," she reminded him, laughing. "And, from my side of the rules fence—no funny business."

He moved into the mainstream of traffic heading north, and gritted the words out. "Right. No weddings. No babies. No doin' the frisky thing for Lucy Miles and me." Yep. He was certifiable. The psychedelic getup she still wore must have turned his brain. How else could he be so annoyed, left somehow wistful by her words? "No kissing. No touching. Just friends."

That adorable wild-rose blush was back, filling her creamy cheeks…and it set him on the fast track to insanity with the urge to see how far down it went, to taste her petal-soft, rose-and-porcelain skin until she cried out in passion for him…

"That's right. Just friends." Determination laced her words.

This was a nightmare…it had to be one of those dreams where nothing made sense. And any second now a Mack truck would crash through the convertible and the alarm would go off. "Um, Lucy? Who's going to be your dark stranger? On the dance floor," he edified when she frowned. "You know, the guy you kiss."

She flushed. "I won't be doing that one at all. I was never going to. I shouldn't have told you in the first place. I only did to show you how banal my dreams are."

"Why won't you do it?"

Looking at him as if he'd grown another head, she said curtly, "You might be the play-around type, but I'm not the sort of woman who cheats on her fiancé."

A long, shamed silence followed. In a life where girls and women had lived to please him, this girl, this stranger, had read him one hundred percent. He was a play-around kind of guy who wanted to play with her, even though he knew she was engaged. What sort of loser did that make him?

A loser who suspects that she's unloved and neglected by everyone in her life, including the said fiancé. But that didn't make it right for him to even want to tempt her—and no one knew that better than he did, raised in a family filled with old-fashioned commitment and love. He might have played around with women, but he'd always done so honestly. Until now…

Her voice startled him back from his unwanted moment of self-realization. "Even if I'd decided to go ahead with that, it couldn't have been with you."

He sucked in his top lip. "Of course not. You don't even like me—why would you kiss me?"

"It's—it's not that." She waited until he'd turned at the sign for Minchin Hills, heading for home, before she answered. "You're not a stranger now, Ben, and—well, catalysts remain untouched by the experiment. They don't change."

*Okay. Count to ten…all right, twenty…*but he'd reached one-fifty, and had turned in at the driveway before his Georgian-style home on the waterfront before he spoke. "And?"

"And—" oh, help, the adorable, drive-him-crazy blush filled her face again "—the outcome of the chemical reaction shouldn't be with you." The blush grew, spreading down to the gentle swell of her breasts. "I couldn't cheat on Hugh, even if—" Though she skidded to a halt, he all but heard the rest of the sentence. *Even if he neglects me.*

So serious, yet so sweet…how come she made him *hurt* and want to laugh at once? How could she make him forget all the rules his old-fashioned, loving family had brought him up with, in just a few hours?

No! It's not the Curse. I won't let it be!

She was his total opposite. For once, he'd met a woman as far out of his reach as the moon, a woman who showed no signs at all of interest in being with him. He had no chance with her even if he wanted to, and if her fiancé didn't exist.

Yeah, she seemed to fulfill those parts of the Curse—but that didn't mean it *was* the Curse. He liked her, felt a depth of tender attraction he'd never known—he might even care about making her happy. It didn't mean he was in love! He was a nurturer by nature, and she reminded him of a puppy that had been kicked around too long to know that the kicks were hurting her.

His silence must have unnerved her, for tears were pooling in her eyes. "Um, maybe staying here isn't such a good idea. M-maybe I should just go home."

"No!" He wheeled around to her, but backed off as soon as he saw the startled wariness on her face. "There's no problem here. I wouldn't make a move on you. We're going to be friends, right?" Trying for lightness he grinned at her, even though the effort hurt. "Hey, this is just fun and games for a week. A few dreams come true. I've got the time and place, so why not?"

She didn't smile in return. "I'm engaged, Ben."

"I know." Serious suddenly, he picked up her bare left hand. "So why don't you have a ring?"

She bit her lip, and fiddled with the buttons on her cardigan. "I...um, Hugh needed money for his experiment...."

It hurt like a physical sock in the guts to speak as normal, but she loved the guy. "He sold it for his experiment?"

"No. I, um, I never got a ring." She must have seen the gathering darkness inside him, for she rushed on. "He says as soon as he gets the funding, rings are first on the agenda—and a honeymoon, as well. He'd love to be able to afford things like that...." Her voice dwindled as she realized what she'd given away.

Ben closed his eyes, fighting against the demon, but it won. "Tell me you're getting a wedding ring and a honeymoon, Lucy."

The silence lengthened to monstrous proportions.

He opened his eyes, saw her face. "That's what the raid here this morning was for, wasn't it? You want to pay for a proper wedding, a ring and a honeymoon."

She averted her face and nodded. "He's put off the wedding twice already," she mumbled, so low he could barely hear her. "We've been engaged two years."

Without thinking, Ben swore.

She touched his arm. "You don't understand. Hugh *must* put his research first. It's not like getting married before I'm forty, wearing a white dress or a big diamond is vital to life. A honeymoon isn't important to humanity." But her defense finished in a whisper, as if some deep-hidden part of her knew that her fiancé found her less interesting than his work, less attractive than his RNA or DNA, somehow less than worthy of being his wife unless she waited half her life.

"Does he know where you are now?" he asked, keeping his hands away from her and his voice gentle.

She flushed as if he'd criticized her, and shook her head. "I know I should have told him first, but I wanted to surprise him with the money when I got home. He'll be so happy…."

"Won't he worry about you? If it takes a week or two."

She fiddled with the buttons on her cardigan. "He's in a vital stage of his experiment right now. He'll assume I'm giving him space, and be grateful for it. He loves that about me, that I make no demands on him while he's so busy."

His whole body tensed with holding in his reaction to what she'd given away without knowing it. "Do you want to call anyone?" *How long has your boyfriend been too busy to notice you? Will anyone notice you're gone?*

She gave him a valiant smile. "The university library I work at will be annoyed, but I was thinking of changing jobs anyway. My parents—well, they're busy, too. And I'm not

lose to people outside the family circle. We—keep to our-
elves, you know?"

Gently, he took her hand and led her into the house, re-
easing her as soon as she sat down on the sofa. "If Hugh gets
vorried, your parents will tell him, anyway," he soothed.

"They don't…" She trailed off, her eyes wide with horror.
'Oh, no, last night's dinner! I didn't call our parents. Oh,
hey'll be so upset with me, going to the restaurant and wait-
ng…and Hugh told me—twice!—to put it off, and I forgot!"
She lifted stricken eyes to his. "May I use the phone?"

Wordlessly he nodded, his heart twisted and wrung out
rom the life she'd shown to him with her words.

Poor, neglected little Lucy. Her heart was sweet and frag-
le as blown glass, and it had already been stomped on too
nany times. She needed a friend, someone who wouldn't
nake any demands on her. Someone had to step up to the
late, give her the fun her starved heart craved, who'd just let
er be Lucy—and it sure didn't look as if there was anyone
lse in the team to volunteer.

She rushed to the phone and dialed a number. Within sec-
nds she wore that look of sick distress on her face he had al-
eady grown to hate so much; but, helpless, all he could do
vas listen in, and gain another sad revelation, another un-
vanted insight into the life she led.

Chapter Five

Lucy felt her anxiety grow with every number she punched in, but Ben was right. Even if Hugh still didn't know she'd gone—and he probably didn't—he deserved to know where she was.

Hugh's phone was answered by his most devoted assistant. "Hello, Jennifer. It's, um, Abigail. May I speak to Hugh?" She sighed as Jennifer rabbited on with the usual spiel. "I know he's busy. Yes, I appreciate that his work is at a vital stage. I won't take a moment. Please, Jennifer, just get him for me?"

Sensing a presence behind her she turned. Ben's eyebrows lightened from the scowling frown he wore, and he smiled at her.

"Abigail? Where were you last night?"

She cringed a little at the cold, whiplash tone.

A gentle touch on her shoulder made her start. "You okay?" Ben whispered, his dark eyes gentle, concerned.

Encouraged, she nodded, and started speaking. "Yes, Hugh, it's me. I have something important to tell you—"

"You didn't go to Bringelly's last night. Your parents had to phone me to ask why we weren't there. They'd waited for you for over an hour. How could you forget to call them? Was it so much to ask that you consider our parents enough to call off the dinner? Or was this designed to make me look bad for not running out on my work for a social engagement?"

"Oh, don't talk rubbish, Hugh," she snapped. "I honestly forgot—the same way you forget our dinner engagements all the time, and I believe you."

Silence for a moment, and she didn't know if he was ashamed at the true comparison, or merely stunned that she'd dared to speak back to him.

She sighed. "Look, tell your parents I'm sorry—"

"My parents are fine," Hugh said coldly. "It's your parents who are upset. They're very disappointed in you."

Thank you for forgetting us, Abigail. The cold, creeping hand touched her soul, her longtime unwanted companion twisting her heart. Oh, how her parents' withdrawal when she displeased them *hurt,* even after a lifetime experiencing it.

She drew in a breath, conscience fighting the voice in her mind, whispering to her that neither he nor her parents deserved to know about her win. "Hugh, I have some news—"

"Can't this wait until tonight? We've had a truly unique breakthrough here this morning. A scent we'd never thought to try made two chimps relate—"

She interrupted him desperately before he went right off on his favorite tangent. "I'm in Queensland."

"Don't be ridiculous. You wouldn't even know the way. You've never been out of Sydney in your life."

The impatient words stripped her bare of any lingering excitement, or even the hope that he'd understand. "It's not ridiculous, it's the truth. I'm in a place called Minchin Hills, on the Gold Coast. I have news—could you please listen to me?"

"I can see I'm speaking to Lucy again," Hugh sighed. "What do you want me to do *this* time to make Abigail come back?"

"I don't want anything from you!"

"You always want. I won't play these manipulative Jekyll-and-Hyde games with you. Now excuse me, I have work to do."

At that, she let the stored-up wealth of neglected anger speak for her. "Well, you're not alone. I'm sick of coming second to experiments and your professors. I'm tired of being ignored."

"Fine. Jennifer was right—you're not the woman for me. You're nothing like your parents—you don't care about anything but self-gratification! The wedding is off—permanently— until you decide to behave like the sensible Abigail that I love."

The line clicked. She turned to Ben, desperately trying to hold it together. "He—he broke up with me."

Ben saw the shimmer of tears in her eyes, bright and misty as corals against her pale skin, as she turned to him. He took the receiver from her drooping hand, and hung it back on the wall. "Give him time. He'll come around."

"N-no. He meant every word. He doesn't want me unless I'm sensible Abigail Miles." She gulped so hard it was visible. "I don't think he'd have looked at me at all if I weren't Professor Miles's daughter. I—I always wondered. I mean, why else would he want someone like me?" Her lips trembled; the tears overflowed, splashing onto her cardigan. "I've ruined my life." She looked at him, dazed yet determined. "I have to conduct this experiment with you. It's the only chance I have of getting rid of Lucy, and winning Hugh back. Will you help me?"

She looked so sweet, so lost. He wanted to comfort her so bad it was a physical ache. But she was confused and distressed, and only a lowlife would try anything with her. "I said I would, didn't I?" But darn it, what kind of a loser was Hugh to not want Lucy? And why couldn't she see it was Hugh who needed to win *her* back?

"Ben?" She frowned, and chewed on her lower lip. "What if the experiment backfires? What if Lucy wins?"

He caught the hand fluttering at him, holding it between his own. "Would that be so bad, if that's who you're meant to be?"

Her fingers laced through his in unconscious appeal. "You don't understand. If I lose Hugh, my parents will—will—I don't know anyone, have no friends outside our world. I don't know what else to do. I don't know where to go…."

He couldn't help but respond to her need, her craving for comfort, for human touch. He put an arm around her and hugged her close. "Hey, it's not that bad. You know me now."

"Oh, yeah." Her smile wobbled. "You're my friend." It was almost a question, so tentative and shy.

"Absolutely," he said, smiling at her. "And remember, if we have to split all this, your options will be wider next week."

But the tears puddled up again. "I just w-wanted enough money for my wedding, and to fund Hugh's research. I—I thought I could make him p-proud of me for once…."

He led her to the sofa and hauled her close against him. "He'll change his mind. Just wait. If he doesn't come to you, I'll go find him, and kick his germ-free butt for hurting you."

She lifted her face and smiled. "Thanks, Ben." She said it as though they were longtime friends. As if it were the most natural thing in the world for him to hold her and caress her hair and give her comfort. As if she was grateful for uncomplicated affection from anyone at all—even a near stranger.

Her tumbled curls tickled his face. Her breath fanned his cheek. Every movement of her body, burrowing in for the comfort of human contact, left him in stronger need. It seemed so natural to kiss her right now—and he wanted to so bad….

Controlling himself was the hardest thing he'd ever done. A simple cuddle was burning into his psyche, a nuclear holocaust on his hormones. This thing between them wasn't a mere volatile chemical reaction, it was major fission. Without even knowing it, Lucy had launched the most potent assault on his senses he'd ever known. Touching her didn't end the fantasy—it only fueled a need for more.

"So when do we start?"

The words took a few moments to penetrate—with the way she moved against him, her breath quivering against his skin, it was no wonder. "Huh?" he murmured thickly, dazed with lust. Oh, yeah, he'd *start* any time she wanted…

Her gaze lowered. "Sorry. I know I shouldn't ask, but you did say I could have a ride, and—"

He pulled himself together. Innocent Lucy. Of course she wasn't thinking what he was thinking. She didn't have a clue how much he wanted her, and if she found out she'd be halfway back to Hugh by now, the selfish jerk who didn't seem to care if he hurt her, so long as he got his way.

She's free now, his heart and body whispered.

Don't even go there. Not unless you're sure you really want her. She's been hurt enough. Just be her friend.

He'd be the best friend she'd ever had—good enough to do whatever it took to stop her returning to her old, neglected life. If it was a bike ride Lucy wanted, a ride she'd get; if Lucy wanted a friend, she had one. He'd bring her every fantasy to life, to show her she was way too good for a loser who only wanted to change her.

If she needed to grieve for her engagement while they played, that was okay. And if she had to go back to her boyfriend and her pristine world next week, he'd let her go with a smile and a wave. Just her good buddy Ben. "Sure." The word that came out so easily three hours before now emerged scraped and rusty. "You might want to change out of those things first."

She laughed a little. "You really hate these poor old pants, don't you? Not to mention this." Plucking at her cardigan.

He grinned. "Hey, Lucy-babe, what can I say? Pink and green hould never be seen, without another human in between?"

"I'm not always so color-blind. I just saw my ticket natched yours, packed and changed without thinking, and vent." She yawned. "Would it be okay if we go tomorrow? 'm half-asleep. I only got to the sweepstakes office at four nis morning."

"Fine by me. Have a sleep," he murmured, his imagination unning rampant, pheromones and testosterone created by ne ten thousand. Pretty Lucy, flushed and disheveled, wear-ng almost nothing, lying across the bed… "I'll order dinner n," he croaked.

"Thanks." She picked up her suitcase, not noticing the lecks of dirt and mold falling onto the carpet with her every tep. In her crushed, lurid green culottes and butter-marked ardigan, tears still in her eyes and her suitcase falling apart n her hands, she marched up those steps with the regal plomb of the Queen of Sheba. He felt giddy, intoxicated, illed with a rush of feel-good oxytocin and adrenaline just vatching her.

Okay, so she's cute, I like her and I feel sorry for her. It's he makeover, that's all. I feel good about helping her, and she asn't got anyone else who cares about whether she's happy r not. A project for the week, before I go on to Monilough nd start my new life.

Liar, his mind threw at him. *You like her, just as she is. The 'project" is your excuse for spending time with her, because ou can barely remember the last time you met a woman who kes you for you, and not what you do.*

Well, somebody had to like the poor kid, just as she was. Didn't look like anyone else in her life had ever found her to e good enough; and if he got something out of this week, nen they both won.

It didn't have to mean a thing beyond that.

"Um, Ben?"

He refocused to see her standing uncertainly at the top o
the steps, wringing her case handle in her hands. "Hmm?"

"Which is my room?"

Volcanic, oceanic, mercurial Lucy. From flaming fury t
earnest scientist and sheltered, vulnerable woman-child, cut
and adorable within an instant—and every mode lit his flam
and turned him inside out with sweet, sweet tenderness
"Mine's the first on the left. There's three others. The first o
the right has its own bathroom."

More shreds of her suitcase fell to the carpet as she twiste
the handle. "Thanks. I'll take a shower before I sleep. I coul
use a long, cool rinse off, you know? It's not this humid i
Sydney. I'm so hot…."

A sudden ball lodged in his throat. Why did she have t
say that, conjuring such graphic images in his overfertile im
agination? Pheromones to testosterone, and he was hard an
hurting. *Not hot for me, not hot for me… I'm her friend. Jus
her pal, her experiment catalyst.* "Ah, yeah, sure," he replie
gruffly. "Take your time. It's only two o'clock. We can orde
pizza for dinner when you wake up."

"That sounds lovely. Thank you." One quick, shy glance
then she turned toward the stairs. "Oh, and Ben?"

"Hmm?"

She threw him a little smile over her shoulder. "Yo
called me babe again. Demeaning term. Sexual objects
Remember?"

He grinned, sending her a mock salute. "Got it."

With another sphinxlike smile, she vanished into her room

Ben laughed as he got out the Yellow Pages, looking u
speedboat-driver hire and certain other equipment rental for th
day. He checked out a few more special places while he wa

at it, planning some surprises for her throughout the week—things to make her forget that her life had fallen apart today.

And, given how many times she'd left him spinning in a four-hour period, he couldn't help wondering what weird and wonderful surprises she'd have in store for him this week, too.

Chapter Six

The light of a fiery sunset pouring in through her west-facing window woke Lucy. A dull, thumping headache knocked on her skull in strange, unsyncopated rhythm. Rap-rap…rap. Bang-bang-bang! Rap…rap-rap! Then it faded to blessed silence. She sighed and rolled over, taking her pillow to cover her eyes.

"Hello-oh! Anybody home? Pizza! PiZZA!"

She opened her eyes. "What…? Where am I?" Squinting against the reflections of gold-rose-and-violet light caressing fresh, whitewashed walls and lace curtains, she knew this definitely was *not* her rather dull-looking inner Sydney bed-sit flat, decorated with bits and pieces from secondhand stores and garage sales.

The luxury sweepstakes house on the Gold Coast. Ben Capriati. Hugh had dumped her. And like Alice tumbling down the rabbit hole, she'd tumbled into a strange new life.

"Pi-ZZA! Yo! Anybody home? Last chance!"

Her stomach growled. "Wait! I'm coming!" She leaped out of bed and hit the floor running.

The sound of pelting water filled her ears as she passed Ben's room, and an off-key baritone. "Babe. I got you, babe..."

Ben in the shower. Ben naked. Dark hair streaming wet. Curls of steam rising around his superb body...

She tossed her sleep-mussed hair to clear the unwanted image, bolted down the stairs and threw open the front door. "Sorry about the wait—"

"Who-o-oa. Don't sweat it, mama. You're worth it!"

"I beg your pardon?" She hung onto the doorknob as she took in the vision before her: a boy with piercings in every conceivable orifice. Eyebrows, nose, ears, lip. His spiked hair was four shades of green, leading to black at the top of a furious Mohawk. The fingernails curled around the pizza box were painted black, like the liner around his eyelids. And over all this sartorial eloquence, he wore a standard red-striped pizza-delivery uniform?

Disoriented, she demanded, "You have pizza?"

The boy's eyes wandered down to her feet, and back to her face. "Two. Man, that's gotta be the best nightie I ever saw!"

"Um...what?" Bewildered, Lucy's gaze followed the boy's, and she gasped. Instead of her culottes and cardigan, she wore her nightie—a thigh-high, creamy silk piece that revealed as much as it hid. She was facing a Marilyn Manson look-alike in a pizza uniform *in her honeymoon nightie?* She vaguely remembered shoving it in with her packing, and blessed its presence this afternoon because she was so hot. The first time she'd ever worn it, and this kid sees her. Typical. Whoever coined the term *luck of the Irish* had never met her.

Embarrassed, she scuttled behind the door, flapping an uncertain hand at the boy. "Go away. Shoo." She grabbed the pizza boxes, jumped back and slammed the door in his face.

"Hey!" The door shuddered with the fists hitting it. "You've got the slip for my next order in that. I need the address!"

She found it, and slipped it under the door. "Now go away."

"You haven't paid me for the pizzas!"

She was down to her last fifty dollars. Sighing, she put the pizzas on the hall stand, found her handbag beside the sofa and slipped the money under the door. "Put the change through the mail slot, please!"

After a moment the bills drifted down; the coins clinked on the tiled floor. "Please, can I see you when you're dressed?"

Of course, he yelled it. She peeked out the window. *Please, don't let half the neighborhood be standing outside, watching....*

Of course they were. Murphy's Law applying with a vengeance.

Dropping the curtain, she backed off, carried the pizzas to the kitchen then bolted upstairs to get dressed before Ben saw her dressed like this and got the wrong idea. With a tiny sigh of half regret, she opened her dying suitcase for a modest out-fit, with a complete set of decent, modest underwear. The most *Abigail* clothes she had.

But somehow, she couldn't make herself do it. Agonizing over the decision, she ended up in a simple, pretty sundress she'd bought for Hugh's lab's New Year's party.

Hugh never even noticed the dress...or anything else I bought to be pretty for him. Feeling rebellious, she walked into a mist of her favorite floral perfume and pulled her hair into a clip above her neck, leaving wild tendrils curling around her face.

When she bolted into the kitchen, Ben was on his favorite stool, waiting...and the heated look in his eyes gave her a surge of feminine confidence she'd never known before. "I knew you'd be even more beautiful in the right gear," he said softly. "The dark red dress makes you look like a wild rose."

Feeling the blush stain her cheeks, she looked at the ground instead of the superb fit of Ben's jeans, or the dark tank top that showed off his upper body. "Ben—"

He angled his face to where she could see him, and smiled. "Hey, I'm a guy, Lucy. Can't expect me to *not* notice a gorgeous woman when I see one."

At least one man wants to look at you.

She looked up, and knew the smile on her lips was shy, touched with the sensual awareness she'd give anything not to feel. "The pizza must be getting cold."

"I put it in the oven." With his face still twisted at that odd angle to keep eye contact, the smile became a grin. "I am that domesticated. I'm not the total barbarian you think I am."

"No, you're a pirate," she murmured, smiling down at him.

Ben straightened and laughed ruefully. "Oh, great. I've gone up the evolutionary scale, from a caveman Neanderthal to Bluebeard. You sure know how to make a guy feel great, Lucy."

"Errol Flynn is more like it," she replied, still without thinking it through; her mind was busy on other things. *A male with a sense of humor,* that naughty imp inside her whispered. *An excellent trait to have in the straitlaced and serious Miles genetics. And the pecs are pretty good, too....*

The fingers tilting up her face were so gentle, she didn't notice—but the look on his face when she lifted her gaze, all sweet and hot at once, she couldn't deny. "Thank you for saying that, Lucy." He kissed her cheek; then, like the touch of butterfly wings, his mouth caressed hers.

Trying to hold her knees up from imminent collapse, weak from head to toe with the potency of one kiss and the sweetness of being in his arms, her brain refused to make the synaptic connection to her mouth, even to say, "You're welcome."

The look in Ben's eyes was shaken, as if the kiss had affected him, too. "Oh, man, we're in trouble," he whispered.

Lucy felt a blush creep down her throat, and she nodded.

He released her waist, and the brief stab of regret at the loss of his touch shocked her. "Maybe we should eat before the pizza dries out."

"Umm—yes. I am hungry." Barely knowing what she did, she touched her lips with her tongue, tasting his kiss on her mouth.

"I'll get the plates." Ben watched her tasting his kiss with her tongue, talking about hunger—and just like that, he was grinding down to a pulp. A fission-blasted pulp, sucked into explosive proportions with the power of one barely there kiss, and her undoubted reaction to his touch.

He'd be a goner if he didn't get out of her proximity fast.

If they ever truly kissed—and he knew *that* held lower odds than his winning another sweepstakes—the consequences could be terrifying. Some deep, man-with-running-shoes-on instinct warned him that for once, he wouldn't have the girl—she'd have him. She'd own him, body and soul. Lucy's love slave.

Then she'd walk away to marry her brilliant geneticist, and he couldn't do a thing to change it.

After thirty-one carefree years he thought he'd escaped the Capriati fate. Until he met darling, quicksilver, rainbow-shaded Lucy, who was already inspiring him with dreams of sitting on rockers beside her in fifty years' time, minding their grandkids.

Except her grandkids will belong to Professor Prissy-chicken—and she'll be alone on that rocker because he'll be too busy with his test tubes or rats or whatever he uses, to even know the kids exist. Or Lucy.

Didn't matter, because she loved the guy—and long ago, Ben had sworn that he would never follow Papa's example of finding love. Making moves on another man's fiancée ranked right up there with running off with your bride's best friend.

The Capriati Curse made the men in his family act like lovesick fools for the rest of their lives and he was nobody's sucker. Yeah, Lucy was adorable—so what? He'd met loads of girls that were—

Like Lucy? Yeah, right.

It made no difference if she was the most unique woman he'd ever known: she was engaged. Fini. Kaput. End of story. Committed heart and soul to becoming Mrs. Dr. What's-his-name, even after the guy had dumped her. Like he was committed for the next five years to a life few city girls could handle.

And anyway, getting married is at the end of the five-year plan, not at the start of it. Sure she's a cutie, but I'll meet another Lucy in time. When I'm ready to fall in love.

But somehow, the proposition felt hollow.

"Mmm…this is delicious," she mumbled, her mouth full of pizza, her lips glistening from the olive oil drizzled over them. "What kind is it?"

The strange mists cleared from his brain. He looked at her, fascinated completely by her simple act of eating, and the irresistible sweetness and budding trust in those big Irish eyes, made him fall in just a bit deeper. *Man, she's so beautiful, so damn adorable.*

He shrugged and laughed as he moved to join her, needing to get past his morbid thoughts. Denial was his only lifeline, so he grabbed hold of it and ran. "Barbecue chicken and bacon." He picked up a slice, careful not to touch her. "I've been thinking. Maybe fate's giving us a message that we got things the wrong way around with our experiment," he said to prod her, to see how she took it. "Maybe you're the real catalyst for all of this."

"I don't want to be a catalyst!" she cried, her face filled with sudden panic as she threw down her food.

"Aha!" A brow lifted. "So you *do* want to change?"

"Yes—no! Not my life…just me," she finished lamely, resting her chin on cupped palms, the utter picture of dejection. "I always seem to be a disappointment to Mother and Father and Hugh. I feel so frustrated when I start dreaming, then nothing comes out of it. I have to learn to be happy with what I have. I have to be Abigail—all the time."

He held a sigh in. Abigail—ick. "Then we'll have to see what we can do to start fulfilling your dreams tomorrow morning."

"What are we doing? Where are we going?" She bounced up on her stool all over again, her voice breathy, her eyes glistening bright. A soft flush of excitement filled her cheeks and throat.

From prim, starchy Abigail back to fun-loving Lucy in milliseconds. He never knew where she'd be next, what she'd say or feel—and he loved it. Hooked, lined, another sinker in place. *Somebody get me a life jacket!* "I booked a boat driver and ski equipment for the afternoon. But in the morning, I've got a surprise for you. Wear something light, with swimmers beneath. Oh, and if you want a sunrise bike ride on the way, leave your hair loose. You need to fit into a helmet."

"Okay." An enormous smile spread across her face. She didn't even argue, which showed how far she'd come in less than twelve hours. "I love surprises." She peeped up at him in the adorable way she had. "You've been so kind to me today. Thank you so much. You're—a good friend already, Ben."

Flooded with wistful tenderness, he cupped her cheek in his hand. "I hope I am, Lucy. You deserve a good friend."

She blinked, looking touched. "What a lovely thing to say. Thank you, Ben. I'll remember that when I'm back in Sydney."

Oh, *sheesh*. The simplest things she said put cracks in his heart a mile wide. "Lucy—"

"This surprise for tomorrow isn't something awful, is it?"

Unsure if he was hurt or relieved by her change of subject from the personal, he sighed dramatically. "Woman, you have the most untrusting nature. But I forgive you. Now let's have our pizza, and hit our respective sacks. We have a big day tomorrow."

He watched her with a smile as she danced her way around the bench, so unconscious of what she did. The adorable dreamer inside Lucy seemed in no danger of being swamped by stiff and starchy Abigail at this moment.

Chapter Seven

Just before daybreak the next morning, Ben sat on a kitchen stool and watched the stairs, waiting for Lucy.

For a guy who was normally jaded about women, his excitement caught even him unawares. But he couldn't wait to see how she'd react to his plans for the day. He wanted to watch her lively curiosity and intense joy as they explored each one of her sweet, harmless fantasies. He wanted to know what more he could do to keep the sparkle in her eyes, the sensuous flush down her throat…like last night, after that moment's kiss. The kiss that still knocked him sideways every time he thought about it.

His time with Lucy seemed defined by tiny, meaningful moments that changed his life and heart, his perception of how life could or should be—and whether he liked it or not, every moment in her company changed his preconceived notions of having any control over his destiny.

He'd even dreamed of her last night. The vision of her in

bridal lace woke him up in a cold sweat—and he didn't know if it was because she was Hugh's bride, or his.

If this is the Curse, I'll fight it all the way. I won't be like Papa and Nonno, making a fool of myself over a woman. We're worlds apart—and soon we'll be cities apart. I won't let myself fall in love!

He glanced up as she rounded the corner into the kitchen, and despite his resolve, he caught his breath. Oh, man, he was in trouble bad. How else could he be hard as granite in seconds for a woman who wore an I Love Mickey T-shirt, her hair a loose ponytail threaded through the clip of a bright red baseball cap?

It's the shorts.

He'd always been a leg man…and as she bounced in front of him in those denim cutoffs, he noticed Lucy's—all the way to her shoes.

He normally loved 'em long and slender and brown with high heels—elegant and sensual legs belonging to a woman who knew the score, who played the game for all it was worth.

Lucy's legs were small and fair and more shapely than slender. She was bouncing from foot to sneakered foot in her excitement for the coming bike ride. She probably didn't even know there *was* a game, let alone a score.

And he'd never felt so aroused in his life.

"Are we going?" Lucy's big eyes fixed on his in childlike inquiry. She bit the corner of her lip in excited anticipation.

He touched her nose, pressing it down. "I've got the bike and helmets ready, and a picnic breakfast. Just tell me when and where you want to stop. I have a place in mind if you don't find one, so don't worry, okay? I just want this to be your choice."

"Thank you." Her voice was shy, her smile half-bitten. She crossed to the garage door and opened it with the set of keys she refused to let go: a subtle reminder of the only reason she was here with him now. "Crabs?"

"The only way for us to go." He pulled her close enough to get through the door, and they edged through together. "A man could get addicted to this sort of entry and exit," he murmured huskily, loving the feel of her against him.

She flushed and wriggled to get away…and then he realized. Oops. She didn't want to know how bad he wanted her.

He forced a grin. "Hey, I'm just a normal guy reacting to a pretty girl touching me. You're a woman of science—these things happen to men. Pheromones to testosterone in seconds, remember?" He moved to the light switch. "Now, fess up. How long have you yearned to ride a powerful engine like this, the wind in your hair, sun on your face, flying without wings?"

Still standing a few feet from him, she wrinkled her forehead, taking his banter literally. "You know, I don't know? It seems forever. I remember waving to bikers as they passed our car when I was a little girl. Even when my parents chided me for my low tastes, I'd give sneaky little waves to them. Oh, how I wanted to ask for a ride. They always seemed so—free."

"That's because they are. Bikes are the ultimate in freedom, Lucy. This will be an experience you'll treasure when you're a dear, white-haired old lady polishing hubby's petri dishes and washing out his chimp cages." He flipped on the light.

"Don't make fun of—ooo-oh!" Her gaze fixed to the bike, she touched the handlebar in something near reverence. "Oh, Ben!"

He knew how she felt. The perfection of line, the fathomless black paintwork, the softness of the muted sky-blue on the wheels, the soft silver of the Ohlins suspension—this Aprilia was tasteful, elegant, poetry in motion—a bike with soul and heart as well as speed. "She's not bad, is she?"

"She's beautiful." She spoke in a reverent hush, a trapped child aching for freedom. "Are you sure you don't mind taking me out? I don't want to damage her."

Lost inside the beauty of her rapt expression, he replied gruffly, "I've carried heavier loads than you on Jan here."

Her eyebrow lifted. "Jan? Is this another mythical girlfriend?"

"Nope." He grinned. "I named her for Jan Brady."

She gulped down laughter. "Why not Marcia, Marcia, Marcia?"

He shrugged, self-conscious. "I guess because I always had a thing for Jan. I never liked Marcia much—she was too showy and obvious. Jan was complex, but she was *real*—that's what made her gorgeous. My Jan's the same. Not the flashy top-line model everyone looks at—aka the Harley you wanted a ride on. Not the little kid everyone thinks is cute, aka motor scooters. She's Jan, and she's perfect just as she is. Maybe she's overlooked by some, but I appreciate her."

"Wow. I'd have thought you'd be a Marcia kind of guy, for sure. Going for the obvious assets and bright personality." She looked at him with a puzzled frown. "You're deeper than first sight indicates, Ben. Strange, but interesting."

He'd never thought about it before, but she was right. He'd named the bike Jan Brady, having spent years with an enormous crush on the more complicated Jan instead of Marcia. Why was that, when he'd gone for the obvious girls of the world ever since?

Jan was ten thousand miles away, and safe. But if you'd ever met a Jan in real life, you knew you'd be on your knees in hours, and your life plans would go out the window.

Well, now he'd met one, and he was still standing—sort of. And that was the way it would stay....

He shook his head to clear it, then lifted the spare helmet from the shelf behind the bike. "Ready to go?"

She pulled off the cap, took the helmet from his hands and fixed it over her thick mass of tumbled curls. "I surely am."

He hopped onto Jan, and after a second's almost visible hesitation, she snuggled in behind him. "Let's hit the road."

He roared out of the garage. She fell back, squealing in half-fearful delight, then she wrapped her arms around him so tight he could barely breathe—and he loved it.

Throughout the twenty-minute ride south, she didn't complain of the cool wind against her bare skin. Nor did she shiver, even though she must have felt the drop in temperature that came with the morning ride. She didn't speak, like every other woman he'd taken on Jan. No yelling commentary about the bike, the ride, the sunrise to their left just starting to touch the trailing clouds with threads of soft rose and gold, lighting the lapping waves with tips of silver fire. He never had to tell her about leaning angles. When he compensated for the lean she flowed with him, as if she was an extension of his body. She never mentioned stopping anywhere for food, though with her healthy appetite she must be starving by now.

He'd never met a woman like her, one who could relinquish control in unfamiliar territory, yet remain so totally herself, comfortable in the adventure, living the experience without fear.

And her boyfriend wanted her to be something else?

He roared in at a spot he'd recently discovered: Snapper Rocks, south of Rainbow Bay, at the southern tip of the Gold Coast. They arrived at the parking lot just as the sun burst into life above the ocean's horizon, gilding twenty miles of sand and clear ocean in glittering rose-gold flame and mysterious shadow.

Lucy gasped.

Ben twisted around to look at her. She'd pulled her helmet off. Her eyes glowed; her cheeks, though they must have been hilled, were flushed. Soft sounds of delight issued from lips arted in wonder as her gaze traveled the water, the sand, the ow of Norfolk pines on the next hill. Even the high-rise partments littering the coast were tinted with a peach-pink ush, almost part of the beauty rather than intruding on the erenity of sunrise.

Without a word Ben led her to the top outcropping of ocks. She climbed up the rugged path in silence, barely seeming to notice what she did until they stood at the hanging edge f rock, the breeze touching their faces and the waves crashing under their feet. "I've lived in Sydney all my life, ten miles om the beach, yet I've never seen anything like this. I've ever come so close to perfection before." She smiled up at im. "Thank you for giving me this experience."

"It's cool." Swallowing a lump in his throat, he forced imself to ignore the fiery need to pull her close and cover er mouth with his. "I love sunrise and sunset rides, too. It's ke being a part of the glory."

"That's exactly how I feel. Ben, I..." She flushed and bit er lip. "I'm sorry I've turned your life upside down, but—but ve never had anything all my own, you see," she said, her tone vistful. "I wanted those prizes so much. To have some control ver—over the wedding, and the ring, and my experi—um, to ave a say in things I want to do with my life. You know?"

"Yeah. I know." His gruff voice hid the fact that his heart ad become total mush. Poor, neglected little sweetheart...

"I guess, well, I just never expected to find a friend under ese circumstances. I never dreamed I could storm into your ouse, threaten to take your prizes away and you'd understand, and give me friendship instead of anger. And this bike de, and—oh, I don't know...but you're a really nice guy. hank you," she finished in a rush and turned away, frowning hard out to the glowing horizon.

Ben stood stock-still beside her, unable to answer. H heart had leaped right into his throat, blocking his breathin;

Now he knew why he'd seen so much beauty in Lucy. Th same reason he'd named his bike Jan, and why he'd never fe a thing for the pretty but basically plastic nightclub babes wh had filled his social time until now.

Lucy had *soul:* life and fire and spirit. She found such jo in new experiences. She knew nothing about him, what he di for a living, didn't care about his status in life, except the a tempt she'd made to talk him into doing a course to improv his lot. She liked *Ben,* not what he had or what he could d for her.

"Thanks," he finally got out. Wanting to hold her, touch he so bad it became a real, physical ache inside his gut.

Still looking out at the rose-and-gold-and-indigo ocean, he face glowed. "It's so nice to share this with a friend, isn't i It's something to remember when—" She stopped there.

He stood beside her in silence. Why ask if Hugh had eve thought of hiring a bike for her, if he'd shown her a sunris or sunset? It was as pointless as asking why she wanted t spend her life with him, when she could have any other gu she wanted—

Including me?

This was nuts! Within a week he'd be tired of her, like ever other woman he'd met. This was desire, pure and simpl Lucy was the first woman in a long time who hadn't jumpe at him at the speed of light, and it heightened the attraction

God forbid that I fall victim to the dreaded Curse. I' enjoy being with her, have a week to remember and say goo bye with a smile at the end...and keep my prizes, my heart an my carefree bachelor's life, all intact.

But the truth hit him like a sucker punch in the heart. A this moment, winning Lucy—with her sweet innocence, he adorable fantasies, her wide-eyed trust and generous soul—meant more to him than his freedom, his career, even all the glittering prizes he'd been so thrilled with just twenty-four hours ago. The prizes she wanted to take from him to fund her wedding to Hugh, a man who didn't even love her enough to call her by her preferred name.

"Give it up, fool. Thinking won't change a thing," he growled to himself.

"Hmm?" Lucy rested her head back against his shoulder, a friendly gesture without sexuality. "What was that?"

You're everything I never thought I'd find in a woman, Lucy. Marry me…

He skidded to a shocked mental halt. *Are you losing your mind? She wouldn't take you over the boyfriend—ex-boyfriend—even if you were serious about asking her. Face it, she loves the guy. Ben, old pal, for once in your life the girl's walking out on you. She needs nothing from you but for you to be her friend.*

Oh, man, I'm turning into Papa and Nonno, obsessed before I've known the girl a day!

He pulled himself together. *Denial, denial! It's not happening to me. It's not happening to me…* "Nothing important. Ready to go on? It's almost seven, and my stomach's reminding me it's about time we got this picnic going."

Lucy sipped from her thermos mug of rich mocha coffee, the midmorning sun warm on her skin, the breeze touching her face, the long blades of grass tickling her feet, and gave a long, drawn-out sigh of bliss. Just as well she was only here a week. Going out for almost every meal, even for breakfast and coffee, could definitely become addictive.

Being with Ben could definitely be addictive.

No! She couldn't possibly be in danger in this short period of time. Not even after that tiny kiss—

After that *incredible* kiss.

It only lasted a moment. One second couldn't change her life, could it? Of course not. She'd been with Hugh six years and she'd had loads of kisses...*just none lately*. It was just one more kiss, that's all. She barely knew Ben. Even if he had a crazy magic in him that called to the wildness hidden inside her, it couldn't compare to what she and Hugh shared. She and Ben were two chance-met friends with—with recreational activities they liked to share. They had nothing in common in their *real* lives.

How can you be sure? You don't even know what he does in his real life.

No! This was just like a Roman holiday. They could be adult about the prizes they both wanted to win, and make the best of a bad situation. If she thought about Ben a lot, it was only because she was having so much fun. It wasn't—

Somehow she had to make herself become sensible and modest again, if this was what her wild side did to her! If she let herself dream, to think any of this could be real, Ben would have the advantage in the prize declaration.

That's it, remember the sweepstakes prizes and the wedding.

"Hey, Lucy, what century have you crossed into?"

Lucy blinked and reoriented herself. Right. She was on an early-morning picnic breakfast with Ben on a quiet, grassy part of the coast, after the sunrise bike ride. Lying together on a blanket four feet apart, never moving closer or daring to touch. Did he still feel last night's kiss as much as she did?

"I'm not sure," she said slowly.

"Maybe you're still hungry. Want another Danish?"

"If I do, I'll never fit into my wedding dress."

"So let it out." Ben shrugged those broad shoulders clad in

a muscle-hugging singlet top, showing off his gorgeous olive form, like the hero in *Strictly Ballroom.* "If you're hungry, you should eat. You're such a tiny thing, what does it matter if you go up a size?" He dug out a Danish from the cardboard box holding their food, and held it out to her in almost as seductive an invitation as the smile on his lush, Mediterranean mouth.

Stupid as it was, taking that Danish seemed almost like an act of disloyalty. "Hugh likes me this size." She tucked a wayward curl behind her ear as the breeze stirred her hair. "We keep fit together."

After a moment Ben put the spurned Danish into his mouth and licked his fingers, slow and thoughtful and oh, so sensual. "We could use a curtain ring, you know. Or we could go to the flea markets and buy one of those faux rhinestone things."

She stared at him. "What are you talking about?"

"You know, a fake engagement ring." His gaze met hers, filled with wry knowledge. "So when you feel threatened by me, you can hold it up in my face instead of chanting *I'm getting married* or *my wedding dress* or *Hugh* all the time."

Oops. She wrinkled up her face in rueful acknowledgement. "Am I that transparent?"

"I'm not going to attack you, Lucy." He looked into her eyes, his filled with hurt. "I wouldn't seduce you, or even try to tempt you while you feel committed to him. I wish you could trust me."

Oh, why couldn't she control that silly blush of hers? "Ben, I didn't mean to—to—you've been so kind—"

A scowl came down on his face like thunder. "No, don't apologize," he muttered savagely. "Not when you're right." He got to his feet and stalked three paces off, jamming his fists into his jeans, and stood there looking down at her, dark and brooding. "I'm not saying it, but it's what I'm thinking, and you know it. That kiss last night—did you *feel* what it—" With an effort that was visible, he dragged in a breath and grinned at her. "This is too intense for a play-around, beach-bum kinda guy like me. Want to do something nuts?"

Breathe, Lucy... Feeling as if she'd been frozen into place, she slowly released the breath she'd been holding as she gazed at him, awestruck, dumbstruck. Did she—could she have that much effect on a man like Ben?

Don't think unless it's rational—and thinking about Ben could never be rational.

She made herself smile back. "What sort of nuts?"

For answer, he tipped the contents of the box out, tore the box into two big pieces, wrapped them both in enormous plastic garbage bags, tied them up and held one out to her. "Do you trust me?"

Without hesitation she took the cardboard. "Lay on, MacDuff."

"Run." He took off toward the edge of a nearby sand hill, and without asking, she followed him. "Jump onto the board and slide," he yelled once they reached the top.

"Sand surfing!" she squealed in awed delight.

They dived onto the fast-sliding boards and flew down the hill of pristine white sand, tumbling at the base on a soft, warm cushion beneath a cloudless near-summer sky. They grabbed their makeshift boards and staggered back up the hill, breathless and laughing.

It took about a dozen tries, but she finally landed at the bottom ahead of Ben. "I beat you! I beat you!" she cried, doing a little war dance of victory.

He chuckled and picked her up by the waist, whirling her around in the air. "I declare the winner—Lucy Miles!"

She laughed in the sheer joy of being alive, spinning around in his arms. "I'm the winner! Me! I finally won something!"

"Yeah," he said huskily. His eyes were dark, his mouth a

twisted slash. "You won." He lowered her, careful about making sure they didn't touch; then he tripped over the cardboard and they tumbled down together. He moved like lightning, and their physical contact lasted only seconds, but she'd felt what he wanted to hide from her. And oh, the tense, brooding look in his eyes, the lack of a comforting joke, told her he felt something far deeper than a simple physical reaction to touch. Right now, Ben was light-years away from a play-around beach-bum kinda guy. It was a good thing women didn't show physical desire so easily…she could make a very big mistake.

She had to call the sweepstakes office as soon as she could to force the issue, before she did something very, very stupid.

Lucy bolted back to the bike, wishing she could go home to Hugh and her quiet, ordered—*it's not boring, it's not!*—life in Sydney. But she had to follow this experiment with Ben to the finish, or Lucy would keep popping up, ruining her relationship—*what relationship? He dumped you!*—with Hugh forever. Then he'd end it permanently, her parents would never speak to her again—and if Ben ended up winning all the sweepstakes prizes, she'd have nothing at all.

Chapter Eight

"Wheeeeeee!"

She was flying! Skimming along the surface of the water in the afternoon sun two miles out to sea, lifting off and landing. She slammed into Ben every ten seconds, but never fell off. Salt water sprayed into her eyes, and her hair slapped her aching face—aching because of the permanent grin etched there.

So what if she wasn't water-skiing? Riding on the enormous pillowed air beds called ski tubes was the greatest fun she'd ever had! Why, why had she wasted two hours trying to get on her feet? Oh, she was so glad Ben kept this as an all-day excursion, changing the boat's booking until the next day. She'd needed that long, just to give up on her stubborn, foolish little dream.

"Just remember to keep your knees hard together. C'mon, Lucy, you can do it," Ben encouraged her, time after time; but when the boat took off, he'd slide with easy grace to his feet, while she'd perform an ungraceful splits, lose her skis, let go of the rope handle and fall face first into the ocean...again.

After a long, lazy barbecue lunch on Stradbroke Island, Ben suggested getting out the tubes when it was clear she'd never make it to her feet on skis. She could almost kiss him for that…

No! One kiss could change your lovely, ordered world!

It already did, the imp whispered smugly.

DON'T THINK ABOUT IT!

After a fun-filled hour on separate tubes, Ben's tube began deflating, so now they were sharing one wide, rectangular tube.

"See? One-handed, Lucy." With a cheeky grin, Ben let go of the handle.

Promptly, she emulated his action. "Big deal, Capriati."

He twisted around to face her—no mean feat at the speed the boat maintained. "Lucy, look at yourself—you're a wild woman, fulfilling your dreams. Could you have imagined yourself doing this, just three days ago?"

She twisted to face him, almost losing her grip on her handle. "Imagined, yes. Believed it? Never. But I am…thanks to you. I'd never have done any of this without you."

With a quick snapping sound, Ben released the tube from the boat. "Hang on tight," he yelled as they spun around and around. "We're in the middle of the ocean, just you and me and the sunshine. We can do whatever you want. I thought this might be something you'd like to do." From the big, net bag hanging off the hook of the ski tube, he pulled out two pairs of flippers, two snorkels and masks. "You ever snorkeled before, Lucy?"

She bit her lip and smiled, touched beyond words. She hadn't even told him about this dream….

Ben smiled at her, that warm, understanding look, and she knew he'd read her emotions with the uncanny accuracy he'd had with her from the beginning. "Snorkeling it is. I've done this a few times, so I can show you how it's done. And don't worry about the driver. I told him to come back an hour after I released the tube. I think that should be enough for your first time. The reef's protected, so don't worry about sharks. There's not much bright coral here, but the sea life should be fantastic."

The tube slowed to a soft roll, following the low, rippling waves. The late spring sun laved their bodies in a soft blanket.

No one could see them but the odd squalling seagull. They were in their own, beautiful world. And Ben had given it to her. "You must be getting so bored with me saying thank you."

He touched her nose. "This is the best fun I've had in years. I don't need thanks—I want to be here. Trust me."

"This is the most fun I've had, ever," she confessed breathlessly, trying to give him what she could. "This time with you has been the best fun I've ever had." *Like the honeymoon I'll never get...*

He pulled out a shirt of his. "Put on a shirt before you go in. You're so fair skinned, you could get burned without knowing it, and be in agony tonight." He handed her a bottle of sunscreen; and while she applied it to her face, arms and legs, he pulled out a tube of zinc cream, and smeared her nose with the thick protection.

Laughing, she did the same for him, and slashed a line down his right cheek. "The mark of a pirate, Captain Capriati."

He dotted some on her cheeks. "Appropriate decoration for a wild woman, Lucy Miles."

And for some crazy reason she got all breathless, and made a silly mistake. She looked into his eyes...to find him looking right back, deep and hot and needing. It held, and held—then as if they both recognized the danger at once, they laughed, pulled on their flippers and masks and dived as one into the warm ocean.

And in the water, she found an incredible inner harmony—

ll her landlubber klutziness disappeared. She swam beside
Ben, the flippers making her feel like a mermaid. For the first
ime in her life she really felt as if she belonged somewhere.
As for Ben, he swam with all the easy grace of a dolphin. They
wam almost as if their bodies were in sync with each other.

Had she and Hugh ever been so—so—

*Don't! This is an experiment, pure and simple. Ben feels
sorry for you, that's why he said that about—about—what did
he say? Does he want me…?*

Then Ben, between submerging and instructions on holding
her breath and releasing the bubbles before resurfacing, pointed
out a school of bright fish right beneath them, and Hugh, her
parents and even the experiment to rid herself of Lucy was con-
signed to the dark recesses of her fading conscience.

"Wow. You weren't kidding when you said you keep fit."

Ben's sides heaved from the long early-evening run along
the foreshores behind the house. His throat needed fluid, even
his lungs felt dry—but his skin was coated in sweat. Lucy, on
the other hand, while flushed and damp, looked as if she
could go a few more miles. She smiled serenely as she used
her sweatband to dry her forehead, then she tugged her ponytail back into place. "No, we—I—run most days. Either in
the morning in the local park, or at lunchtime."

With Hugh.

For the past two days, he could almost see the unspoken
word hovering in the air like a sentence inside a cartoon bal-
loon—like the tangible presence of her ex-fiancé hovering between them wherever they went.

Wasn't that the way it should be, for a woman in love?

Then why did this feel all *wrong?*

Because *Hugh* was all wrong! If he were Lucy's fiancé, he
wouldn't be hanging around with his germs and gene strands,

RNA and DNA. Saving humanity was important—hell, he
was a doctor, he understood the importance of the job—but
he, Ben, would at least have heard Lucy out, no matter how
busy he was. And if he'd learned that some other guy was
making her dreams come true, he'd have dropped everything
and been up here on the first flight after her call. He'd have
muscled his way into the house, standing, sitting and lying beside Lucy at all times, reminding the other guy and the whole
damn world just who she belonged to. He'd be making very
sure that if Lucy had any unfulfilled dreams, he'd be the one
to give them to her, because risking losing Lucy to another
guy would never be an option.

If he were Lucy's fiancé, which he was not and never would
be—because his gut instincts told him that if he got himself
in any deeper for Lucy than he was now, he might just set a
record in the stakes of Capriati insanity over a woman.

*Two days. It's only been two days, and already you're in
way over your head. You have to stop this!*

And suddenly, he knew what he had to do: he had to get
her boyfriend—ex-boyfriend—up here, and fast, before he did
something really stupid.

Why wasn't Hugh *here?*

*Because he didn't listen to her long enough to know what
was going on. And until he does know, you're cheating him
just as bad as if you* had *seduced Lucy.*

"What's on the agenda for dinner tonight?" she asked, rubbing her legs down with a towel—giving him a superbly unconscious view of her cute butt.

He shoved his towel in front of him to hide his usual hot
reaction to her. "You like seafood?"

Her moan was almost an animal growl as she straightened
up. "I *love* it…and oh, it's been months since I had any!"

"I never met a woman who loves food like you do," he

eased her, remembering the first night's intense reaction to
he pizza, her pleasure with the Danishes yesterday morning.
Even with the simple hamburger at lunch, she'd been in ecstasy. She'd eaten more than he had at the barbecue today.
'You get excitement out of food the same way other women
do with—clothes or makeup," he finished, sounding lame, but
he couldn't use double entendres with Lucy. She either missed
the point, or it just plain embarrassed her, and gave him the
guilts.

She laughed. "I know. Why do you think I run every day?
I swim in summer at the local pool, too. I have to burn off the
amount I eat."

"Seafood it is, then. I'll book a place while you get ready."

"I need a shower, long and cool. I'm so hot." She groaned,
stretching backward, then she straightened and grinned. "I'm
a physical being, I know it. I love stretching and showers and
running and swimming almost as much as I love food."

His gut ached, his groin throbbed and he was suffused
with heat from head to foot, watching her stretch. It was un-
believably sexual, watching as those sweet little breasts lifted
high, the creamy skin translucent with its rosy afterglow.

*Bad choice of words, Capriati. Flushed from exercise is
more like it!*

As soon as she'd gone upstairs, he booked a restaurant;
then he stood there, trying to physically force himself to walk
away as his hand hesitated over the phone like a hovering conscience. How could he continue the experiment if he did this?
Would Lucy be thrilled or horrified? She was having so much
fun now…

*And you're going crazy with temptation. So get the guy up
here. Lucy loves him—and that makes him a visible barrier
against temptation, and might keep you from becoming another Capriati Curse victim.*

Feeling low, almost immoral, he grabbed Lucy's walle from the hall stand. She had about a dozen of the guy's card in there. *Dr. Hugh Carmody, geneticist. Michelson Labora tories, Alexandria, Sydney.*

He dialed the number before he changed his mind.

And true to form, Lucy's fiancé was there, even at seven at night. It took about nine rings before he answered. The Per fect Man's radio-quality voice sounded cool and abstracted and was all Ben expected. "Yes?"

"Dr. Carmody?"

"Yes," Hugh replied, impatiently. "What can I do for you?"

No wonder Lucy looked distressed when she talked to the guy, if he used this kind of belittling tone on her. "My name's Ben Capriati—"

Hugh sighed. "And this means something to me because—?"

Squelching the desire to say, *Well, I was going to fund you to the tune of a million dollars if you were nice to me,* he counted to five and said, "I have news for you about your fi ancée, Lucy Miles."

"Oh. Right." Another long-suffering sigh came down the line. "It's ex-fiancée, actually, but go on. I might as well know the worst. What's she done now?"

"Actually, she could have won a prize on the sweepstakes if you're interested."

"Abigail never gambled in her life. She can't afford it Now who are you really?"

"I told you. My name's Ben Capriati. Until two and a half days ago I was the undisputed winner of the Lakelands Chil dren's Charities Sweepstakes number 224. But *Lucy*—" he couldn't resist the slight emphasis on her chosen name "—discovered she had a matching ticket, and went to the sweepstakes office. She's up here in Minchin Hills now, staying in the house with me until the legal winner and who gets compensation is announced."

A short silence. Then Hugh spoke, his smooth voice harsh and impatient. "I don't know where Abigail picked you up or how much she's paying you for this rigmarole, but it's patently ridiculous since she was with me in Sydney three nights ago. She can't have gotten herself up to Queensland in a day—not in her rusted rattletrap of a car. I've got no time to sort out this play for attention of hers. I have work to do."

A simian scream shattered Ben's eardrum, then the line went dead.

Ben stared at the hapless receiver with loathing, too mad to care that he was talking to a dead line. "You jerk. Monkey-loving geek. Dr. Dolittle wanna-be. What makes her love you so much I don't know, but if you don't get up here, I'll—"

A tiny sound made him spin around. In trepidation, he looked up to the staircase...and he saw Lucy wearing only a bathrobe, white-faced and with damp, tousled hair. "What did you say to him? What have you done?"

He ran up the stairs to her. "Lucy, I—"

"You shouldn't have called him," she whispered, shaking. "Don't call him names like that."

"Lucy, I'm sorry if I upset you, but I thought I owed it to him to let him know—"

One lifted hand silenced him...or was it the sad, stricken look on her face, as if he'd betrayed her? "It—it's kind of you to think of bringing him here for me." Tears filled her eyes. "But you don't understand. He—he meant what he said. He doesn't love me, not the way I am now. I think it's over. He won't come, all right?"

"I'm sorry," he said quietly. It was all he could think to say, besides the words and emotions that were clearly taboo.

She sniffed and dashed at her eyes. "Did you call him to

get rid of me?" she whispered. "I know I can be a real pest, but—but you suggested this experiment. If—if I'm annoying you, I can just stay in my room and not bother you."

Idiot! Why not shoot yourself in your other foot and be done with it? "No, Lucy, that wasn't it at all. I swear to you, I'm enjoying your company and all the fun we're having."

"Okay." She bit her lip, not looking very convinced at all. "I know we've been having fun with this experiment, Ben, but don't interfere in my life. You can't judge what's right or wrong for me on two days' acquaintance."

Shamed, he could only nod. So used to a career that demanded snap diagnoses about what people needed, he'd done the same in an emotional way to Lucy. But she hadn't asked for help. She didn't need his opinion—or interference.

"I'd better get dressed." She turned away without looking at him. "Did you book a place for dinner?"

Almost sick with relief that she was still willing to stay, he said huskily, "Yeah. This place does fantastic barbecued seafood, right on Broadbeach. We can do a moonlight walk on the sand after, if you'd like."

"Sounds lovely." Her voice was husky, too. "I'll be ready in twenty minutes." She disappeared into her room.

He had a second chance—another chance to show her—

She doesn't want you, and she's a for-a-lifetime, Capriati Curse kind of woman. Stay friends—just friends.

Chanting the inner mantra that helped no one—least of all himself—he stalked to his room to change.

The restaurant was dark and intimate, candlelit, with massive plate-glass windows looking out over one road to the wide-open beach and the warm brightness of a thousand stars above it. A band played quiet, romantic ballads in a shadowy corner.

And Ben was making her feel oh, so gloriously nervous….

"Every man in the room is jealous of me tonight, Lucy," he said softly as they touched glasses of a semisweet white wine. "You look incredible in that dress, with your hair like that."

The butterflies in her stomach all but blocked out her normal healthy appetite. Unable to tear her eyes from his, she sipped her wine. In a sky-blue cocktail shift dress that suited her coloring, with her hair half pulled up around her head, loose curls tumbling over the hidden clip, she did look her best tonight, but she'd been brought up to believe that she'd never be able to compete with other girls. "What a sweet thing to say," she whispered.

He touched her face for a moment. "It's true, Lucy." His smile was rueful. "Even guys like me can be sincere."

Nerveless fingers almost dropped the glass. Her eyes wouldn't obey her command to turn away from the deep, hot look in his eyes…

"You have the calamari. I noticed how much you like it." Scooping up the final pieces on his fork, he placed the food in her mouth with the fluid sensuality that seemed to belong to him. Again and again his fork parted her lips, feeding her.

"Aren't you eating?" she finally asked.

"I'm having far more pleasure from watching you." He watched her every mouthful, from main course to the rich mocha mousse she ordered for dessert, his eyes hot, possessive on her. Of its own volition her hand picked up a spoon, and she fed him, too.

Always a passionate eater, never had chewing and swallowing felt this intimate or sensual…so lush and rich on her tongue. On the lips his spoon caressed while her spoon caressed his mouth, and his deep chocolate eyes turned her insides into honey.

"Good?" His dark, silky voice was low and warm as the night, caressing her with the same lush intimacy.

The butterfly wings fluttered lower in her belly. "A-are you seducing me?"

"Could I?" His tone, filled with the velvet of midnight in summer, made her think of tangled satin sheets...

Trying to find sanity, her gaze dropped a little, but it landed right on his mouth. She wet her lips with her tongue, wishing she were a different kind of woman, one who could play the game, taunt and tease him, but the only words that came to her were truth. "If I was ready for this...if I thought you meant it for more than one night, or a week, yes, I think you could," she confessed, her voice quiet. "Tonight, I don't know that I care—but tomorrow you'll want to run, not walk, from the responsibility of being with me. I don't play, Ben."

Slowly she felt a trembling hand being lifted, caressed by his smiling mouth. "You think I don't know that?"

As if they had a mind of their own, her fingers turned, drinking in the feel of his mouth. Her eyes grew heavy with the overload of sensuality, and closed. Yet her mouth tumbled out words that had nothing to do with the sleek, hot fire of arousal in her belly. "Are you being kind, because you think I need it after Hugh was cruel to me?"

A gentle piano solo filled the silence. Then his lips moved against her fingers. "I wish I could say that's all this is—but I can't. God help me, Lucy, I can't. I've never wanted any woman the way I want you. Ever."

Sweet, sweet aching bloomed through her body at the raw, stark words. She had to believe him now...and oh, it had been so long since a man wanted her—and it had never, never been like this. Yet still her rebel mouth spoke through her heart, against her body's need. "I can't do this, Ben. Part of me wishes I could—part of me wants to so badly—but I can't."

He only smiled at her. "I know. You might be free, but your heart isn't. You're safe with me, Lucy. Nothing will happen with us until you want it to." The old-fashioned seduction of "Unchained Melody" wafted across the room. "If I asked you to dance, would you dance with me?"

Wordlessly she lowered her hand into his.

When they moved together on the warm, dark, crowded dance floor, unspoken déjà vu flowed through her, an inevitability as sweet and addictive as melted chocolate. Her dark stranger held her with delicate care, as if she were precious porcelain, yet close, so close to his heart—and she didn't even try to stop him, because she wanted it, too. Her head fell to his shoulder; her hand around his neck crept up into his hair without her knowing, sliding silky strands through her fingertips. Her feet worked in time with his, slow and dreamy, like harmony and symphony; her arms held him as if they'd never let him go. Her body, long awakened, thrilled to the aroused state of his, the gentle hands whispering down her spine to her hips, moving her even closer. And like untamed magic, a spell put on her against her will, her hand pulled him down to her, her lips seeking his. "This is crazy," she whispered, "but I can't stop it."

"Do you want me to stop?" he whispered back, almost touching her mouth with his own, hot hunger filling his eyes.

Hers drifted shut. "No."

A whisper, almost a groan, drifted to her. "You're killing me, Lucy." Then, at last, oh, at last—because she hadn't been waiting for this for only a day, but her entire life—his mouth claimed hers.

A whole lifetime she'd waited, oh, so lonely, hungry for human contact, for simple caring—and one touch, one incredibly tender kiss, a touch of moonlight and starlight and *sweetness,* made it seem as if all those years she'd spent alone in the dark had never been, and never would be again.

Oh, this was what she'd missed, what she'd *hungered* for,

all her life…and her kiss on a crowded dance floor moved from unfulfilled dream to surreal, magical reality. She moaned softly, and pulled him closer. *More, Ben, oh, please, more…*

Later, much later, he pulled back to frame her flushed face in his hands, his eyes dark with emotion. "Wow. That was—unbelievable. It's never been like that before. You take my breath away, Lucy."

Oh, the glorious feeling of feminine power that gave her—because she knew he wasn't lying about the effect she had on him, her dark, dreaming pirate. "I barely know you," she whispered between kisses: soft, clinging kisses, like gentle raindrops that, one by one, filled her needing soul with shining joy. "I don't know anything about you."

His forehead touched hers; he smiled into her eyes. "You know me, Lucy," he whispered back. "You know *me.* The rest is just a story. Filling in blanks."

She thought about it. Was he right? The essential soul of Ben, even though he'd told her so little about himself—did she know him? Somehow the thought frightened her.

Probably because you feel like you've known him all your life within a few days, and you still feel like your own parents and fiancé are a mystery you can't solve…

She couldn't let him go if her life depended on it right now, but her wavering heart demanded she make him stop. "This is insane, Ben—it can't be real. We've only known each other a few days."

"I've told myself that a hundred times," he groaned into her hair. "This is dangerous—intense and beautiful and scary as hell."

He was right—it was beautiful—and too strange, too new to her. Too intense. It was dangerous, and while she'd always hungered for adventure, it never involved her heart. *That* she had to keep safe. "I'm not ready for whatever this is," she faltered.

He froze, even while still holding her with that lovely, addictive tenderness she'd never known. Yet his eyes had lost that hammering dark need, leaving only sadness. "Is this Lucy speaking, or the woman your family wants you to be? Why, Lucy? Why are you willing to stake the rest of your life on a man who demands that you change who you are to suit him? Why are you killing off an important part of yourself to get him back, when he might only want you for the money you give him, and a prissy act you put on? Do you really want to settle for a man who isn't proud of you, just the way you are? Why do you value yourself so low, to accept the scraps he throws you and think he's right when all he does is hurt you?"

His words cut her like a careless knife. Was he right—did he put too low a value on herself and her own happiness?

You're not a girl who will attract many men, Abigail, dear, her parents had told her more than once. *You're very lucky to have caught the eye of such a genius as Hugh Carmody.*

"I wish I could answer you," she mumbled through a huge lump in her throat. "But I don't know who I am right now, or who I want to be, or what I want. All I know is, I can't keep living like this."

"I'm a fool. Why don't I just open my mouth wider and put both feet in at once?" Suddenly he gathered her against him, holding her with exquisite care. "Of course you're not ready. You've had too many changes in the past few days. I promised I wouldn't push, yet here I'm doing my level best to panic you into running back to—to Sydney."

To Hugh.

The unspoken word jerked her back from the edge with a frail grip on sanity. How pitiful was this, that the name of the man who'd dumped her like an unwanted kitten was the only protection she had against potent magic of a man who was— who had to be—all wrong for her. Who would take her well-

ordered life in Sydney and turn it upside down and inside ou
"Maybe we should go to the markets and get that ring," sh
whispered.

Fire erupted in his eyes for a moment, and she caught he
breath. Then, by sheer force of will, she watched as he force
the flame to tamp down to a slow burn. "If that's what yo
want." His voice was cool. His arms fell away from her.

"Maybe we shouldn't walk on the beach tonight," she mut
tered, struggling not to cry.

His hands balled into fists at his sides. "No. I think we'v
both had more than enough, um, romance for one night."

Romance. It was the one thing she'd always craved in he
life—what she'd had in abundance tonight, thanks to Ben—
yet on his lips, the lush, full lips that twisted as he said it—
the word sounded like a painful epithet.

"I'm sorry, Ben," she faltered.

"Yeah, I know." The twisted smile hurt her. "Do me a favo
Lucy. Don't kiss me again unless you mean it. We're suppose
to be friends, and friends don't use each other. I've discov
ered that even a guy like me—the kind of guy you despise s
much, even when I give you more respect and interest tha
your superior boyfriend ever will—can be pushed too far."

She gasped, and felt the blood drain from her face. "I—
I'm *sorry*," she whispered. "I thought—I thought—"

"What?" he asked, his eyes dark and cynical. "That I wa
doing this for the prizes—or for brainless fun? You kee
thinking that way if it makes you comfortable, Lucy. You'r
kind of addicted to that, aren't you? Your perceptions of peo
ple are limited by first impressions and the scientific degree
you see like some kind of a war hero's medal. Heaven forbi
that you actually see the rest of the world—people withou
letters after their names, or doctorates and research grants—
as worthy of your respect."

She took a stumbling step away from him, as if in horror—ut she was more horrified at herself. Though she'd never ought of it that way, he was right. The ordinary people of ie world were like riffraff she'd been kept separate from all er life, and, afraid of the unknown, she'd turned her parents' iild disgust for those outside their pristine world into an art orm. *Coward.*

What could she say? Her mind was blank of anything but elf-disgust. "Ben...I'm—"

"Sorry?" he finished for her. "Yeah, I know. So am I."

Stricken, she turned and stumbled to the table to gather up er things, while he stalked over to pay the bill.

Chapter Nine

Another day, and another experience with Ben that made h[er]
feel as if she could fly…

"That's it, Lucy. Great leaning angle," Ben shouted wi[th]
obvious pride, as she zipped around the small racing track [in]
the soft light of early morning. "You're doing it!"

She laughed behind the helmet, feeling the sheer joy [of]
being alive. She was flying. She was riding a bike, all on h[er]
own! Ben trusted her with Jan—and she was doing it! Onc[e]
Ben explained to her that a sensible speed helped maintai[n]
balance, she lost her fear. All her squeals were pure exhil[a-]
ration as she made every turn and corner, not with anythin[g]
like precise perfection, but without going head over feet o[n]
the track.

When was the last time she'd felt this happy? Had she eve[r]
felt like this—as though she was walking on air?

Flying in the wind. Racing over the ocean. Going out f[or]
breakfast, lunch and dinner without counting the cost. Walk[ing]

ng on the beach with a man who didn't make spending time
with her feel like a sacrifice. Just living for each day, without
worrying about anything but enjoying life. Just being Lucy—
and being with someone who liked Lucy, faults and all.

She had three more days. Three days left of being Lucy before she walked away from this part of herself forever…but
at least she'd have this to remember—to know that once in
all her humdrum existence, she'd been a wild woman.

*But will it be enough? Is Lucy fading at all, or growing
stronger?*

No! Experiment conducted; reaction taking place. By this
time next week, she'd be tired of this meaningless if fun-
filled existence. She'd have conquered this wildness inside her
soul and become meek, sensible Abigail again, and she'd win
Hugh back. She'd be so glad to be home again!

*Sure you will. Life's a real barrel of monkeys with
Hugh…literally. Jennifer can no doubt tell you all about it.*

*Why do you want to be with a man who demands you
change who you are to suit him?* Ben's words of last night
haunted her heart, relentlessly repeating over and over, and
yet still she had no answer. Why *did* Hugh demand that she
change? She'd never asked it of him.

*Maybe because he sees how easy it is to manipulate me into
doing what he wants—and because I let him do it. He's
watched Mother and Father do it for the past six years…and
he's seen me cave in, every time.*

She gasped; her hands jerked reflexively. Had she always
been so weak—or had it been years of parental training, making her expect to be neglected, and to be grateful for the little attention she got?

"Lucy! Watch what you're doing!"

She started—what was she *doing?*—but she couldn't correct the extreme angle of the bike, and sort of half slid, half

flew off the bike to the ground, bouncing along the track until she came to an undignified halt at the grassy edge.

"Lucy! Lucy!" She heard the pounding of Ben's feet racing toward her. "Lucy, are you okay?"

"Ooooow," she groaned softly.

"Lucy, talk to me!" He unzipped the thick leather jacket she was wearing for protection, lifted her shirt and probed her ribs, chest and belly for wounds. "Where does it hurt?"

She gulped; her breaths came fast and shallow. She was in pain all right…but not what he was searching for. His touch, oh, so tender along her ribs, her belly, her hips, still felt like butterflies with wings of sensual flame. Hot, honeyed sin against her bare flesh… "I'm fine," she croaked.

"Don't patronize me, Lucy." He spoke with gentle finality. "Just tell me what hurts and where, okay?"

"I'm serious," she insisted. "Just bruised, I think. All the padding you put on me stopped anything serious." With a befuddled grin, she lifted one leg, padded at the knee and ankle.

He stripped off the thick padding with exquisite care, first one leg, then the other. "Just let me check. Sometimes the pain doesn't show itself immediately. Some people have walked miles on an ankle broken in several places."

She frowned. "How do you know?"

He sighed. "I do read the newspapers…and not just the sports section or the funnies. Human health and biology were my best subjects at school, and I've passed the advanced first aid course more than once. I'm not completely brainless, Lucy. In fact, a lot of people think I'm quite intelligent."

She felt a flush fill her cheeks. "I—I didn't mean it like that." But, to her shame, she had. She did think of Ben that way— probably because she was *comfortable* thinking of him like that. Her holiday fun guy, with no comparison to make to Hugh.

Comfortable was rapidly becoming her least favorite word.

He shrugged. "My mate Danny walked over a mile home after a hockey injury when we were fifteen. He was in pain, but it only felt unbearable an hour later. His ankle was broken in three places." His hands, having gently tugged her jeans down, felt along her bones, from thighs to feet. "I can't feel anything."

Oh, but I can....

Could he feel her trembling? Was it written in her eyes, all the sudden hot ache? She had to stop it now, before she made a fool of herself—ruined her whole life—

What life?

I'll stop him—just as soon as I can make my voice work.

"Lucy?" His hands had slowed, hovering over her ankles. "Lucy...?" Voice husky, not daring to finish the question.

She glanced at him for one delirious, delicious moment, saw the need and anguished desire in his burning dark eyes, knowing it was reflected in her own. Struggling to remember all the reasons why this couldn't happen between them.

They didn't matter now. She couldn't remember anything but Ben's dark, raffish male beauty, and a hard, aroused male body that made her wonder if any other man had wanted her so badly, if any man had ever driven her so crazy with wanting...

Lying back in the grass, she tugged him until he came to her, and she whispered, "Yes, oh, yes, Ben."

With a smothered groan he kissed her, deep and sweet, caressing her face and hair with that so-addictive tenderness. As if she really mattered to him. As if she was someone important, and not a nuisance to be placated—

Don't think about it.

He took the kiss deeper, tumbling her on the grass until she lay on top of him. Like last night, she could feel his aroused state, and thrilled to it. When his tongue touched her mouth she moaned, twining hers with his in delicious weakness and heat. This was like a wonderful dream...a fantasy come true with her fantasy man.

Don't touch me again unless you mean it. Even guys like me can be pushed too far. I give you more respect and interest than—than—

Oh, no...what's his name?

Stricken, she pulled away. "I—I'm sorry, Ben. I promised you only last night that I wouldn't do this," she whispered.

"It's okay," he said, frowning. "I asked for it." He jumped to his feet and helped her up, then, with his usual exquisite care for her, got her dressed again. "What's happening with us, Lucy?" he asked, his voice quiet, his eyes serious...galaxies from that play-around beach-bum guy she'd assumed him to be at first.

"I can give you a scientific explanation for what's going on." She looked into his eyes, earnest and sincere. "You know how people call it chemistry? Well, it is. It's hormonal. When two people find—are—well, anyway, the pituitary gland releases pheromones, which have an indefinable scent to the other person that others won't smell. And then oxytocin and endorphins are released, the feel-good hormones, and adrenaline, which adds to the general feeling of excitement. So you're happy being with that person. The endorphin rush, you know?"

"Yeah," he said softly, smiling at her with a sweet, tender version of his pirate's grin. "I know. I get a rush every time I see you, or even think about you."

She blushed and smiled shyly. "Um, thank you. Anyway, see, you might think it's a crush—but what it really is, is the body doing its natural thing, trying to bring physically compatible people together to propagate the species. We can't control this kind of reaction. It's not our fault." She sighed at his melting, hot-chocolate eyes, and her traitorous body's fiery response to the need so clearly written in his face. "I said I wouldn't touch you again unless I meant it. I'm sorry, Ben. I didn't treat you with the respect you deserve."

At that, his smile twisted. "Like I said, I asked for it. Don't sweat it." He looked around for a moment. "Wait here."

Helpless with yearning, she watched him stalk over to the row of vending machines that littered the wall of the club house. He shoved coins in every one, collecting the small plastic bubbles, jerking them open one by one, then flinging them away. After throwing away about twenty of them, he gripped one in his curled fist, and returned to her. "Give me your hand."

She held out her left hand, fingers spread, and he began sliding a cheap rhinestone ring onto her finger. "Now we can't forget."

His eyes met hers, and held.

Oh, no, Ben had to see it, see the anguish in her eyes, the sweet ache of desire she couldn't conquer or even deny—the need to have him touch her and kiss her again—and again—and again. Oh, to be touched, even on the fingers, made her realize how long it had been since anyone *but* Ben had touched her in tenderness. In—um…*oh, heck, the monkey-rat-guinea-pig man's*—case, it had been months. The only times he'd touched her, kissed her, in the past year were when she made it clear she was unhappy again, and he'd placate her in case her parents became angry. And never once had his touch been so exquisitely caring as Ben's, as if she was special to him.

The simple act of Ben buying her a fifty-cent engagement ring made her see all that—*um, monkeys—Tarzan? Oh, no, I've got to stop listening to Ben!*—her fiancé had never done for her in six years, and Ben, her sweet friend, had done for her in four days.

Could she go back to being quiet, meek, overlooked Abigail again after this week, after knowing Ben's care, his touch and kiss? Could she return to meek Abigail, and be grateful for any leftover scraps of time and affection?

Her gaze dropped to her left hand, where the ring still sat halfway down her finger. "Ben, I—"

"You'd better do this yourself." He moved his hand away from hers, and stalked over to check for damage on his beloved Jan as she finished pulling the fake ring on her finger, reminding herself as much as him that she was taken, by—by—*the lab-coat guy*—and that, until four days ago, she'd been so sure—*yeah, right*—that she was deeply, truly, madly in love with—

What the heck was his name again?

"That's it, folks. Hold the fin, and let her take you along with her," the instructor told her.

Lucy floated behind the dolphin in the long, low pool at Sea World, the only place on the Gold Coast with available dolphin-human contact. She was hanging on to the fin of a playful female, reveling in another day of dreams-come-true.

Yesterday, after the bike lesson, they'd had lunch lazing at Surfer's Paradise Beach, then spent the afternoon at Dreamworld riding roller coasters and water rides before eating at an open-air evening market right on the beach, munching on exotic Asian foods as Ben bought her soaps and scents, a Chinese flute and a charcoal sketch of them together.

And now, she was actually swimming with a dolphin…

She could feel sunburn biting into her back and nose, but she didn't want to cover her modest sky-blue bikini with a T-shirt. Not yet. Not when she felt so utterly feminine, so totally sexy every time she turned her head, feeling Ben's gaze on her in heated male admiration for one sweet, fleeting second before he masked his emotions.

"Oof!"

She giggled, watching Ben double over again. "Mikey obviously senses your, um, ego problem."

"He's obviously sensing something!" One of Ben's hands held his dolphin's fin, the other frantically covered his groin as the dolphin he was supposed to be swimming with attacked once more—but this time, as if the creature knew Ben was protecting himself, it hit with swift military precision, flipping its tail into Ben's gut.

Ben doubled over again, his face twisted in comical agony.

"Are you all right?" She tried to sound concerned, when she was trying very hard not to laugh.

He groaned and made one last desperate grab on to Mikey's fin. "Can I please have *one* swim, buddy, without you trying to kill me?"

The dolphin trainer's voice came at that moment. "Thanks, folks. Time's up. If you'd like to have your photos taken with Mikey or Bailey, move to the right of the pool. Next couple, please move into the pool and we'll be right with you."

"Just as well this was your fantasy, not mine." Ben smiled with an air of painful bravado as they waded out of the pool. "I can laugh at this absurd situation."

"So what's your fantasy? We can do that, too, if you like," she offered impulsively, thinking of how hard he'd worked to make her week here a happy one.

His eyes grew hot for one sweet, mad second. Then, just as the tom-toms began pounding in her most feminine, hidden core, he gulped, dragged in a breath and said, "Do me a favor, Lucy—don't make offers like that off-the-cuff to every guy whose house you invade, unless you want a legion of hopeful men following you around the country." He lifted her hand, decorated with the cheap fifty-cent imitation ring. "Don't ask me the question again until this comes off. When that happens, I'll think about what fantasy I want you to fulfill for me."

Shaken to her heart by his words and the glorious sexual taboo neither of them could speak aloud, knocked right out of her fears and insecurities about her ability to arouse a man after years of self-doubt, she couldn't think of anything to say. "Okay," she whispered, like a child.

He gave her a slightly twisted smile. "You're getting sunburned. And don't forget your hat." He bent down and plucked the shirt and cap from her bag. He pulled the T-shirt over her, carefully covering her sunburned areas, then plopped the cap on her head, pulling her wet ponytail gently through the hole at the back. "That's better. Can't have your dreams turning to nightmares with heatstroke."

Stunned, lost, she peeped at her watch to remind herself of the date. It was true. A week ago, she hadn't known this man existed. Five days ago, she'd thought him her enemy, standing in the way of her dreams. Now she knew the truth: Ben Capriati was the best friend she'd ever had.

He even cared if she got a sunburn.

Hugh—that was his name!—would have noticed her sunburn, too, still in a tender way but somehow patronizing, pulling the clothes over her head, telling her she was such a forgetful girl. He smiled on her human foibles and forgetfulness as if he had none himself.

Don't think about it. Forget him for now!

And somehow she found that easy to do when she was with Ben, and she was about to ride home with him on a dream bike, to a dream home, and be with a man that embodied dreams and fantasies far stronger than any prize she could ever claim.

Chapter Ten

"Looks as if the boyfriend has come around," Ben remarked quietly as they pulled up in the driveway.

Lucy saw the offering lying against the front door, and shook her head with a quick pang of hurt. "Hugh wouldn't send me flowers. He never has before."

Ben frowned, looking at the flowers as if they held all the answers to life he didn't want to know about. "Maybe he started."

She shook her head again. "No. He considers it a waste because they only die. He says if I want to look at flowers, go for a walk in a garden." Her forehead wrinkled with a thoughtful frown. "Who could they be from?"

"Only one way to know." With a grin that didn't quite come off, he leaped out of the car and onto the porch. "They're for you. Nobody in their right mind would call me 'the foxy lady in the most bitchin' nightie I ever saw.'" He gave her a curious frown. "Who's Malcolm?"

"What? I don't know anyone called Malcolm, and as for the nightie comment, even Hugh hasn't seen—" She blinked and gasped. "The nightie…oh, the—the pizza boy…he *did* ask to see me when I was dressed…." She groaned, and covered her eyes with her hands. "Trust me to be the one that, when I finally get flowers, I get them from a Gothic punk pizza deliverer…."

"Another dream come true, Lucy-style, huh?" Ben burst out laughing. "This I gotta hear!"

She mumbled the crazy story from behind her hands.

Ben laughed all the way through. "Dang, how did I miss that nightie?" He grinned when she punched his arm. "So Malcolm, the new millennium version of the Scarlet Pimpernel, the Ebony and Emerald Pierced Pizza Jock, takes on Cleo's Most Eligible Monkey Man and the Italian Stallion to win his fair lady's affections. He leaves his gifts in secret, but can Hugh or Ben find him? We seek him here, we seek him there, but always he eludes us. But we don't despair. Tune in tomorrow for another exciting episode of 'We All Love Lucy'!"

Unable to help it she laughed, and plucked the fragrant mass of Australian wildflowers, waratahs, wattle and ferns mixed with baby's breath from his hand; but before she'd done more than draw breath, the force of a sudden sneeze made her reel back against the bricks. "Ah—*choo!* Ah—*choo!*"

Her eyes watered. Her head started pounding. And the violent sneezes went on and on.

"I think we'd better get rid of Malcolm's love offering. I suspect you haven't been so closely exposed to one of these native flowers before." He plucked the wildflowers from her hand, tossing them away; then he opened the front door. "Time for a dose of antihistamine. Come on upstairs. It's in my bag."

She blinked her watering eyes, and squinted up at him. "You carry antihistamines in your bag?"

"Any allergy sufferer worth their salt does in spring." He led her up the stairs into his room. "Grass seeds, wattle and pollen can make your life miserable in seconds. It's a fairly common allergy. Don't sniff your flowers from now on."

She was in his room. He was in the bathroom, where he'd stood yesterday naked, in his steaming shower... "Okay," she croaked.

"Has it affected your throat?" Ben bolted out to her, his face filled with concern. "If your allergic reaction's that bad, you'll need epinephrine or adrenaline at the emergency section—"

Oh, help. Now what did she do—get a shot, or admit the embarrassing truth? "I'll be fine!" She heard the lingering huskiness in her voice between sneezes. "Just give me the stuff."

"No way. This sounds serious, Lucy. Don't try to be a hero. You need epinephrine at least—I can hear how the allergy's affecting your throat already. This could be dangerous."

She stamped her foot. "Just give me it! I'm dying here!"

"That's what scares me!" Ben's voice cracked; he dragged her against him. "I just met you. I can't lose you now. Not yet."

She gaped up at him, seeing that he was one hundred percent serious—and scared. Scared of losing her.

Seeing that raw honesty in his eyes, the vulnerability he wasn't ashamed to show, her resistance and pride puddled in a heap at his feet. "It's not an allergy—ah-*choo!* I—I—oh, darn it, if you must know I was having a fantasy about you in the shower, and—ah-*choo!*—"

"I get the picture." His eyes warm and soft, he chuckled and kissed her forehead. "Thank you for having the courage to tell me that—and thank you for coming into my life. You're a constant joy to me."

"And you're driving me crazy! I need those tablets *now,* Ben! Ah-*choo!*"

"Oops." He handed her the tablets. "C'mon, let's get you

that water." He led her down the stairs into the kitchen, poured her a drink and lifted her chin. "Drink up, Lucy." His gaze was warm and soft on hers, her dark, dreaming pirate. She swallowed the tablets, watching him over the rim of the glass. He was so darn gorgeous....

"You look like a little girl doing that—but the expression in your eyes is all woman. Lucy, what are you doing to me?" he whispered, his face filled with something she'd never had until this week, from anyone—but this was what she'd imagined when she read a certain word in her beloved books. Tenderness...

When was the last time Hugh looked at you like that? Did he ever look at you like that, or was it all in your imagination?

She put down the glass, seeing the subdued twinkle of the rhinestone on her finger, like a tired reproach. "I'm sorry," she said awkwardly, between sneezes.

"Yeah, I know you are. No more than I am." With sudden ferocity he lifted her in his arms. "Am I real to you, or just some brainless fantasy guy to fulfill your dreams? Do you know I've got a heart, a mind and dreams of my own? Do you want to know about me, what I do for a living, where I'm going? Or would that ruin your stereotype of who and what you think I am?"

Stunned at his sudden turnaround, she stared at him, lost for words. "I...like you, Ben," she faltered, wondering what she'd said to make him so fierce, so angry. "I'm trying to be honest with you. I know you're real—and I don't want to hurt you."

Ben closed his eyes, and put her back on her feet. "Yeah. It's a problem, isn't it? We planned a crazy week of fun with no strings—but I like you too much and you don't like me enough. I want more with us, and I can't have it...but the look in your eyes tells me maybe I could—that you want me like I want you. Your kisses tell me it's not just my imagination, that what we have isn't a dream." Blindly he moved his face against hers. "We're in danger bad, Lucy."

She nodded against his hair, inhaling his sun-washed scent with the delicious quiver she'd always associate with touching Ben from now on. "We don't fit together. Chalk and cheese."

"More like waving red rags to a bull. A speeding car without brakes. A runaway train in the night." The gentle murmur quivered into her skin. "It's never been like this for me before, Lucy. I want to make your dreams come true—to be a hero for you—and it scares me silly. I don't know how to deal with it."

"It scares me, too." She sighed and shook her head. "It's so hard. If only—um, you know, the monkey guy—would come…"

"Hugh," he supplied with a fatalistic grin, dropping his hands from her waist. "His name's Hugh. Remember?"

"Um. Ah, yeah. That's right. Hugh, my perfect man." She barely knew what she was saying; she only knew she wanted Ben so much she was shaking. She loved the way he held her, as though she were something precious, and the way he looked at her, as if she was the most beautiful woman in the world—and the way he kissed her made her feel like Sleeping Beauty, waking up after a lifetime of emptiness.

"Is he so perfect, Lucy? Still?" Ben asked, his gaze deep and fathomless on hers. "Is he really the man you want to trust your whole life to?"

She blinked slowly. Had she said Hugh was perfect? And—oh, help, *did* she want to spend her life with him? "I—don't know…."

He turned away, fiddling with the block of sharp knives on the kitchen bench. "You said you met him through your parents, right?"

Safe topic. Take it! She picked up her water glass, and walked over to the sofa. She curled up in a corner, and watched him flop into the big armchair opposite with a strong dose of pique—and another sneeze. "Yes. My parents invited him home one night, about six years ago. He was assisting my father while he finished his final doctorate thesis." She shrugged. "He was the fourth man they brought home, but they finally hit the jackpot. A man who found something to interest him in—ah-choo!—someone like me."

He frowned. "What do you mean, someone like you?"

"You know. A nice, overlooked girl who doesn't attract men on her own," she explained earnestly. "My father explained that I'm not the type to inspire lust, or romantic interest in men at first, or even a second glance…or ever, really. So I needed to find a man who would appreciate my finer qualities."

"Your father's wrong." He slanted her a strange, curious glance. "Which are your finer qualities a man should appreciate, in his humble opinion?"

Oh, dear. She inspired lust in him…? Romantic int—

You know you do. You know this isn't a game for him anymore, or for you. He's right, this thing between us is getting dangerous….

Don't go there. Keep on the safe topic. She sneezed twice more, then, feeling worn-out, tilted her head against the back of the sofa. "My ability to live on my own, and being able to amuse myself without demanding constant attention. My scientific knowledge—second-best, since I didn't inherit my parents' intelligence, but more than most people know. I'm quiet and retiring. I'd keep the home fires burning, and bring up my children as I should." She sighed. "They were so disappointed when I started changing. Becoming demanding. When I showed them, and Hugh, that I needed—um, wanted

nore than they thought." She sneezed one final time, then
miled. "I think the tablets are working now," she said, to
hange the subject.

"Good." A long silence, and she wondered what he was
ninking to put that frown on his face, and the dangerous glint
n his eyes. "What is it you demanded of him? What did you
vant from him?"

She felt the flush touch her cheek. "To be involved with
ne wedding. I wanted him to shop for things with me, like
ne dress or his suit, or for flowers. I wanted him to—to *want*
o marry me, and not put it off again. I know it's selfish, when
nis work is so important," she rushed on. "My parents tell me
should be able to wait, to do it all myself so his work goes
moothly. I have my career to concentrate on, after all. But—
ut I don't like my job anymore, and it gets lonely, doing all
ne wedding preparations yourself, you know? And two years
eems a long time when you're waiting…."

"Yeah. It would. Do you think your request was unreason-
ble, that you were wrong to expect a little attention from the
nan who claims to love you?"

"I—I don't know. Mother and Father said—said—" she
topped there, unable to say it.

He tipped up her face. "It's okay, Lucy. I wouldn't discuss
ny parents with people I haven't known long, either. We're
oth loyal critters—even if our families don't always deserve
t." He gave her an understanding smile. "I know mine drives
ne nuts at times."

But she couldn't smile; for some reason, the gentleness in
nis voice brought a lump to her throat. "Sometimes it's hard,
ust waiting, waiting. Do you know how lonely it is to be near
ne person you—you think is the love of your life, but their
neart's in another place?"

"I don't know if I'm ready to answer that yet." Ben stared

so intently into her eyes she blushed again and turned aside
fiddling with a scatter cushion. "The other day, you said yo
were thinking of changing careers," he said abruptly. "Why?

She felt herself squirm a bit. "I don't know," she confessec
plucking and twisting at the gilt tassels. "The library was
natural progression for me. It's almost in the field of science
Since I couldn't get the marks in microbiology or physics fc
what they wanted—I mean, I wanted to do…"

She started when she felt warmth on her hand. She looke
up to find Ben crouched in front of her, his hand over hers
"Hey, let up on the poor tassel, Lucy, or I'll have to put yo
in to the cushion police for abuse."

She gave a weak laugh, and released the cushion into hi
keeping. Ben put it aside, with a smile. "Now tell me wha
you really want to do with your life."

She bit her lip. "It's—silly. It doesn't make the number
scientifically. It'll probably fail."

Ben just waited, crouched before her, smiling. Waiting
And with a rush of faith, she knew she could tell him. This wa
Ben. He wouldn't laugh at her. *With* her, yes, but never *at* he

And you thought he was a caveman, her imp informed he
smugly.

His fingers caressed the back of her hand, a friend's o
brother's gesture belied only by the melting tenderness in hi
dark eyes as he drank in her face. "Tell me, Lucy."

She smiled, but it was all wobbly. "I want to be a farmer,
she whispered. "An organic grower."

"Fruits or vegetables?"

Her smile grew in confidence as his question showed h
took her ambition seriously. "I have some old data on appl
growing in arid areas. A professor friend left it to me in hi
will three years ago. I'd really like to try it, to see if it coul
work." She took the cushion back, caressing it with her fre

hand, dreaming. "I'd love to get about two hundred acres or so, and grow the right insect-repelling weeds—and not just as a border. I'd love to ride around the property on a horse or motorbike—"

"With an Akubra on your head and a blue cattle dog running by your side."

"Yes," she whispered, rapt at the vision.

"Why won't it make the numbers? What's wrong with the data? Is it because of the salination problem with the artesian water in the Outback?"

She shook her head, frowning. "No, it's not that, because the whole basis of the theory is the trees' being able to adapt to the saline water, using saltbush and the right insect-repelling weeds that actually drink up excess salt. I—I don't know what the problem was, really. Hugh looked at it, and said it was a waste of resources, and to stick to the library. We—we needed the regular money from my job to fund the wedding, and he said it would take funding from his experiment needlessly, when it wasn't going to work, anyway."

Silence. And for some probably silly reason, "Unchained Melody" floated through her head again, along with the memory of the kiss in the warm darkness of the dance floor. She found herself trembling.

"Did he tell you why he felt it wouldn't work, Lucy?"

She blinked. "Um—no. He didn't." Why hadn't he told her the reasons? And why had she just accepted his word? Had she always been so pathetically *passive?*

Isn't that what they trained you all your life to be? Why do you think your being Lucy irritates them all so much?

"It means a lot to you, this experiment, doesn't it?"

His gentle voice broke in on her thoughts. "I don't like working indoors all the time. I've lived my whole life indoors, at libraries, schools, at home. I'd love to work out-

doors, with the sun and wind on my face. And—and it's
something all my own, you know? I know Professor Coleman started it, but I spent over a year finishing the data in
my spare time. I tried a miniexperiment in potting planters.
It's *mine,* my experiment."

"You should find out exactly why he didn't think the data
correlated, Lucy. Maybe there's ways around it."

"Maybe I will," she said, frowning. Wondering again. Ben
the dropout, the guy who did nothing, sometimes spoke like
he *knew*—

*Do you know what I do for a living, what I want to do with
my life? Or would that interfere with the preconceived notions
of what you think I am?*

"You should give it a shot. You said you don't like being
cooped up all the time. Didn't you do any activities outside
as a child? Didn't you do any team sports?"

"I'm a klutz," she confessed shyly, glad to leave the subject of Hugh's betrayal of her wishes behind. "I was never
chosen for team sports. But we had a gym downstairs my parents kept fit in. And we lived near Centennial Park, so I was
free to walk or run there." She shrugged. "But I always felt
lonely…everyone else always had someone to be with. My
parents were always so busy with university and research
work, I didn't like to bother them."

"So when you and Hugh got together, you ran there?"

She smiled and nodded, remembering the first time. The
pride and sheer joy she'd felt, having someone to go to the
park with.

"Have you always felt alone in the world, Lucy?"

The gentle question tiptoed into her soul and opened its
hidden door of sadness. "I don't remember a time when I felt
like I fit in somewhere," she confessed, feeling like a fool.

You never felt loved—not as the person you are. Hugh wants dutiful, repressed Abigail—Professor Miles's daughter, the prim librarian grateful for his scraps of time and attention.

"What about now? Do you feel lonely here with me?" Ben's voice quietly walked inside her aching loneliness, filling it with warmth and tenderness and caring.

"Not with you. I could never be lonely when I'm with you," she whispered back. "I've never felt so glad to be alive as I have this week. You treat me like I'm a princess—like I'm someone special."

He touched her face. "You are special. You're the most special and adorable woman I've ever known."

She looked into his eyes, so deep and dark and hot, and shivered with yearning. "We're all wrong for each other."

He kept his fingers on her face, trailing tenderly, until she shivered again. "Maybe we're the right kind of wrong," he whispered, as if the idea scared even him, her sexy, cocksure caveman. "Two wrongs make a right and all that."

She shook her head, aching, yearning to believe him. "I'm slow and staid. Change frightens me. You move a million miles a minute. I could never keep up with you."

He gathered her to him, and she felt him trembling—*Ben was nervous and unsure?* "I could slow down for you, Lucy. You're worth the wait."

Oh, how she *ached* to believe him—but decades of training held true, and sadness and wistfulness filled her in a tide. "I'm a very square peg, Ben."

"Maybe I'm not as round as you think." He smiled at her. "Ask me, Lucy. I'm just waiting for you to ask."

Oh, how she wanted to ask—*why aren't you round? Why do you think we aren't as opposite as I believe?*—but the connotations of his answers frightened her. Surely nothing so perfect, so special could come to her, staid, plain Lucy Miles? Surely a man like Ben Capriati couldn't *want* to connect to her?

You know he does. That's what scares you so much. You're so used to everyone neglecting you or trying to change you, the thought of someone loving you for you is terrifying.... "I can't," she whispered, shaking. "This…this is too fast for me, Ben."

He bit his lip hard. "What if our 'getting rid of Lucy' experiment doesn't work out the way you want? What if Lucy wins? What will you do then, if you can't be Abigail anymore?"

"I have to be Abigail," she sighed, but the protest was half-hearted, and they both knew it. She didn't want to think about going back to her no-life with—*oops, um, the monkey guy*—and they both knew that, too. But what Ben asked her to believe, could—no, *would* change her whole world.

"Just suppose that happens," he insisted gently. "What will you do with your life?"

She shrugged, biting her thumbnail. "Maybe if I win something out of our crazy situation, I can buy my farm, do a practical experiment instead of working in a lab. If not, maybe I'll get a loan from the bank," she went on, feeling something akin to excitement. Yes, she could do that…she could go to the bank, get a loan and a place, and begin her experiment…. "And—and maybe I could hang out here with you a little bit longer while I look around for my farm," she said softly, teasing him with a glimmering smile. "A week or two—"

"Yeah, hang out with me awhile, Lucy." His voice was gruff as he picked up the poor abused cushion and destroyed it in turn. "Hang out with me a week or two, or a month. Maybe a year or two. Or ten or twenty or fifty years. Just stay with me, Lucy. Stay."

She gasped. Did he mean that? *Could* he…? "Ben…?"

He stilled at her tone. His answering smile was weak, rueful. "We're playing just suppose, remember. And you did ask."

But she hung on to his earlier words like a tenacious bulldog, knowing only that a tide of incredulous joy filled her as he stopped asking, and *told* her what she needed to know. "I— I could really stay? I wouldn't bore you, or annoy you? You wouldn't get—tired of me? Hugh's right—I'm irritating when I get excited about something. My parents say I'm a pest when I get a bee in my bonnet...."

He gathered both her hands in his, caressing them, smiling into her eyes. "How about we conduct another experiment? Hang out with me awhile—say the next fifty years—and ask me afterward if I've ever been bored with you, gotten tired of you or wanted to get rid of you. But I think I know what my answer will be."

Tears filled her eyes as the emotion overflowed into her heart and soul. Oh, this was what she'd yearned for, all her life. Finally she wasn't a bother to someone, and it felt so wonderful...so beautiful and *right* that touching him no longer felt wrong. Her fears took wings. She forgot everything else but the need hammering through her bloodstream, filling her mind, heart and body with sweet heat. "Oh, Ben..." She leaned toward him as he moved to her, his warm, dark gaze locked on hers.

He touched her chin, caressing gently. "Be sure, Lucy. I don't want just a day or two of us. I don't want to be your rebound fling. I want to know I have some credibility with you."

"Your credibility grows every minute," she confessed shakily. She gave in to aching need and touched his face, moving her fingers through that rebellious lock of hair, intoxicated by the tense passion written on every feature of his face at her simplest touch. "That's the problem. I keep forgetting that until the other day, I was, um..."

"Engaged," he whispered.

"Yes." Her gaze locked on his eyes. "I keep trying to think about, um, you know, the guy who hangs out with his monkeys, and...well, I used to think he loved me, but I haven't believed it for a long time. I just held on to it because there was nothing else in my life to hold on to." She ran her fingers through his ruffled, waving mop, thick and dark and beautiful. "But when I'm with you, I don't just forget his name, or what he looks like...I no longer want to settle for second best. I like being Lucy—and you like me as Lucy..."

"Like you?" he muttered. "I'm helplessly and totally crazy about you, don't you know that yet?" He drew her to her feet and wrapped an arm around her waist and drew her closer, his eyes a dark, burning fire. "I can't control this anymore. I don't care if it's the Curse, I have to be with you. Pheromones turned to testosterone within an instant of being near you. Adrenaline and endorphins are running rampant inside. I feel like I can conquer the world when I'm with you, and everything in my world is all right just because you're here."

Lost in a sweet haze of sensuality and *happiness,* she barely registered the odd reference to a curse. "My pheromones have turned to estrogen. The adrenaline and endorphins are alive and flying inside me," she whispered back, wrapping an arm around his neck, her other hand flat on his chest. Their bodies touched, and she moaned in delicious weakness. "Chemical systems locked and loaded."

"With a flaming double-barrel. It's too late now. We're at DEFCON One." Wrapping one of her loose curls around his finger, Ben looked as dazed on overloaded sensuality as she felt. "I think an explosion is imminent."

She gave up the fight and said it. "Kiss me, Ben."

"You smell like sea and sunshine." His mouth moved closer, so close his warm breath made her lips tingle, so close she could inhale the sweet scent of the chocolate honeycomb bar he'd eaten on the way home, as he finished the journey she ached for.

He kissed her with a passion too strong to be pity, too in

ense to be about fun and games. He wanted *her*. Ben Capriati, her dreaming pirate and sexy caveman, was driven to this
wild, unleashed passion by Lucy Miles, prim, plain, old-maid
scientific librarian....

She moaned and moved right into his body, lacing her fingers through his hair, touching the skin of his neck, his ear,
his face while he caressed her waist, her shoulder with growing need, hotter desire. "Lucy, *mia bella*, I want you so bad,"
he mumbled through scorching kisses on her throat.

She gasped and arched back to take in more. "Ben, oh,
Ben." Her hands grasped his face and tilted it up, meeting his
mouth with her own. Deeper, hotter, harder kisses, fueled by
need and desperate desire... "I want you, too, Ben. I have
from the moment I saw you."

He framed her face in his hands, with a serious look on his
face. "Before we go any further, I have to know where we're
going from here. I meant what I said before, Lucy. I'm not
playing here. I don't want to be your rebound guy, or a week's
fling. I need to know I mean something to you. I want you to
tell me what you're going to do about Tarzan."

Oh, that kiss, that magical, wonderful kiss...lost in her
lovely daze, and the pounding tom-toms in her yearning body—
aching as she never had before, and for Ben, only Ben—she
blinked, frowned and whispered, "Who...? Huh...?"

A gentle, acerbic voice crossed the room from the still-open
front door. "Um, actually, I think he might mean me, Abigail."

Chapter Eleven

Lucy swiveled around, gasping. *"Hugh?"*

"At least you remember my name now…that's something." His gaze roamed them, still locked in each other's arms. "You didn't waste much time, did you, Abigail?" The blond, tanned godlike looks of Lucy's ex-fiancé accused her—but they stunned Ben. Heck, he'd been imagining a bespectacled geek as his competition, and he got the pinup boy for science! "I can't believe you'd forget me so fast, after six years together."

"Like you forget Lucy all the time?" Ben muttered to himself, but Lucy's tightened face told him she'd heard.

She wriggled against his arms. Reluctantly he let them fall, and she walked toward the man who had been her fiancé. "What are you doing here? And how did you know where to find me?"

"Maybe we could discuss it in private? Once your new, um, friend isn't listening in." He gave the word *friend* a whole new wealth of contemptuous meaning.

Lucy's eyes flashed. "He *is* my friend, Hugh, and he doesn't deserve your snide comments. If you don't like what you saw, then leave. I'm not answerable to you anymore."

Tarzan blinked. Obviously he wasn't used to Lucy returning fire with fire. Ben grinned. Looked to him like the old boy was in for a few surprises....

She turned to him, biting her lip. "Ben, would you mind?"

He felt his eyebrows flick up. "Sure," he said, with a strong effort at an easy tone. "Jan needs a bit of body work."

"I'm sure she does," Lucy's Perfect Man sneered. "Did Abigail need *body work,* too? Are you part of a harem here, Abigail?"

Ben walked into the garage, resisting the desire to warn Hugh to be careful, under threat of violence. But though he left in silence, he left the door ajar. He had a feeling Hugh wouldn't pull his punches with Lucy, and if he hurt her—

"So, Abigail, what's really going on here?"

The cool, imperious tone set Ben on edge—but Lucy replied coolly enough. "What business is it of yours, Hugh? You said we were over, you don't love me, you don't want to marry me anymore. So if I find someone else, what does it matter to you?"

"It matters, all right?" Hugh snapped. "Answer me, Abigail. What's happening here?"

"I tried to tell you the other day. I'm here until we sort out who won the sweepstakes. How did you know where to find me?"

"And where the hell did that cheap, tacky ring on your hand come from?"

Was this how the guy intended to win her back? Ben, a natural healer, had never wanted to deck anyone as badly as he did now. Arrogant, self-centered, pompous *jerk*—

"Ben bought me a ring to remind me that I was engaged.

He knew I wasn't ready to admit that it was over with us. So he got this." Lucy's voice was gentle, but final. "He knew I needed the security of a ring—because he listens to me. It took his giving me the ring to realize how much I've needed to know, to *feel* that I was important to someone. I wondered if you even remembered who I was at times. I've felt alone for so long."

Finally, the arrogant jerk seemed to recognize he was on dangerous ground. "I'm sorry, Abigail. I should have listened to you the other night instead of snapping at you. I was wrong to say what I did. You *know* I love you, snooky—and it has nothing to do with your parents. I don't want to lose you."

Ben wanted to puke at the patent insincerity of the words. So he'd found out about Lucy's ticket, and understood there was money in it for her—and therefore, for his experiments? *See through it, Lucy. Don't go back to the jerk!*

"How did you know where to find me?" Lucy sounded cautious, as if feeling her way on unfamiliar ground.

After a long silence, he muttered, "Your story hit the paper. A colleague who reads this trash showed it to me."

Lucy gasped. "Our story's in the media? How?"

"I don't know. Reporters and their sources are like squirrels with loads of hidden nuts. The point is, I went to the Lakelands office today to find you." He sounded seriously ticked. "I had to give them four types of identification and find a picture of us together at our engagement party before they would give me this address."

"Why did you come? We both know you don't love me. You were waiting for me to come groveling back to you, and be your meek little supporter again." Silence reigned, and she sighed. "Come on, Hugh. Tell the truth. It'll be easier in the long run."

After a few moments she said it for him. "You want the money for your experiment, right?"

The silence continued. Ben's imagination got vindictive. *'d love to give the geek a frontal lobotomy, and dedicate his nassive and insensitive brain to science....*

"What did you do when you read the article about my win, ook the first flight?"

"I drove up," he mumbled. "I got leave for five days."

"So I wasn't worth coming for, but the money was. I only eserve ultimatums and ridicule—but as the woman who night be worth money for your experiment, I get attention and ealousy and long-overdue declarations of love. You asked for eave to wangle money out of this situation—but you wouldn't ave dreamed of coming just for me. Nice priorities, Hugh."

Ben was amazed at how calm Lucy's voice was. She ounded more analytical than hurt.

"At least I haven't been playing footsie with some cheap iker who has a harem running around the house!" Hugh napped.

I'll give him cheap...at least I don't hang out with monkeys!

"Jan's a *bike*." Lucy's voice wobbled with bubbling laugh-er. "And while Ben and I have kissed, no other woman has een here—and I swear my feet have never made contact vith Ben's."

Ben bit back a startled laugh, and moved to repair the cratches on Jan from Lucy's fall yesterday. Lucy didn't need is protection; she was doing just fine all on her own.

But Hugh's voice got louder and more aggressive, as if he vas determined to make him hear. "I can tell other body parts ave made contact with that man, Abigail! Don't deny it—I aw you all but fused into him just now!"

"I wouldn't want to deny it, even if it was any of your busi-ess—which it isn't." She spoke without apology. "Nothing as happened between us yet—but it will. And you know vhy? Because women need human contact. We need kisses and hugs and to run and play and to feel loved. When we don't get it for long enough from one man, we'll go elsewhere. What you saw then was the third time Ben and I kissed…but it was far from the first time I wanted to."

A little, shocked silence. "What are you saying, Abigail?"

"I've known for a long time that you don't love me, Hugh," she said simply, without any emotion. "I tried to deny it, to keep hoping you did, but deep inside, I knew. I hung on because I had nowhere else to go, nobody to care for me, and the outside world was a mystery I was scared to solve. I wanted my family's approval, too, and being with you gave me that."

After a minute of utter quiet, Hugh said, "You've changed Abigail. You're—stronger."

"Yes. Just having this week with Ben showed me the truth. If I don't take charge of my own life and happiness, no one else will—especially not you." She spoke without apology or compromise. "You don't care about what I want from life. You didn't just make your experiment your top priority, it's been your only priority for two years. Neither you nor my parents have ever listened to me. But Ben cares about everything I say and feel. He respects what I want from life, like my apple experiment, or wanting a wedding dress. Whether it's a big dream or something little, he treats me with the same respect. He's been—a very good friend to me."

Hugh snapped, "And how do you think your parents will feel about your erratic behavior?"

Ben's hands curled into fists; he strode toward the door. He'd make the jerk shut up if he had to—

Lucy spoke before he reached the door. "I don't want to hurt Mother and Father, but I doubt I *have* the power to hurt them. They're not interested in me as a person, only as a reflection of their names and reputations on campus." She sighed. "All my life I've done what they want, what you want, and it hasn't made me happy. I don't like my job, I've waited years for a wedding that isn't happening. I want more in my life. I want to have fun, to play. I like being with someone who likes *me* without issuing demands or ultimatums to make me change to suit his life. I want someone to want to be with me, to spend time with me without it being a sacrifice."

"I see." Hugh sighed.

"When I first came here, I tried to stop this with Ben. I wanted to hold on to what we had, but I discovered there was nothing real to hang on to, because you never loved me, and I don't love you, either. I just wanted to make my parents proud of me by marrying a scientific man." A long, thoughtful silence. "I'm not coming back, no matter which of us wins the sweepstakes. I'm staying here. Ben—" her voice softened at his name "—Ben makes me happy. I want to be with him, for as long as he'll have me."

Happiness crashed over Ben, breaking like waves over the ocean a few miles distant. *Thank you, God, oh, thank you!* He hung on to Jan's handlebar, almost falling to his knees in joy as visions of rings and mortgages and diapers filled his head— and a lifetime of the laughter and joy and the intense passion for living that was Lucy.

"And how long could a girl like you last with a guy like him?" Tarzan's voice just missed being a sneer. "He looks like the kind of guy who changes girls every week."

"I know." She sighed again. "I doubt I'd keep Ben interested for very long, but even if it only lasts a month, I think I'll be happier than I've ever been with you."

Ben closed his eyes, happiness swamped by hurt—hurting for her. *Oh, how they've all destroyed your faith in yourself, my beautiful girl. But I can change that. Just give me the next fifty years or so.*

He'd given up fighting this. If what he felt for Lucy was a Curse, may he stay blighted for the rest of his life. No matter which part of her complex personality she displayed, prim librarian or sweet, wistful child or wild woman, he was on his knees, at her feet. Love had come at last, and yeah, he would do whatever it took—*anything*—to have her with him for life.

"So you think you're in love with this guy after what, five or six days? Abigail, think about this." Hugh's voice was full of urgency. "Yes, I've taken you for granted the past few months, but I'm offering a lifetime. Can you honestly say you'll get that from him? Are you sure you'd want it? You hardly know the man."

"You don't want me, you want my money and my parents' approval and support—and I do know Ben," she retorted, her voice hovering somewhere between stubborn and uncertain.

Knowing what was coming, Ben groaned. Whose stupid fault was it that Monkey-boy had this kind of ammo with Lucy?

"Where is he from, Abigail? Who are his family? Does he have another girl or two somewhere?" He stopped, but Lucy obviously had no answers. "What does he do for a living? Do you even know that much about him?"

"No," Lucy said, in a very small voice.

"This is like a shipboard romance, baby," the jerk said gently. "You've gotten away from home for the first time in your life. You're having fun. You've met someone who likes you as Lucy—or so you think. But maybe he's just out to vamp you until the winner's announced? Have you wondered whether he's charming you just in case you're the winner?"

"N-not for a few days now…" Her voice was so small now, Ben barely heard her.

"Was he angry when you came here?" Hugh asked gently, finishing off his demolition job on her budding self-esteem and confidence.

"N-no…h-he took me out for c-coffee, and a b-bike ride, and—and all nice places, things I want to do…" Her voice wobbled in distress, knowing what Hugh would say next, as well as Ben knew.

"Do you think that's a normal reaction for a man about to lose his winnings?"

"N-no." A tiny sob.

"Abigail, anyone who knows you for a day will find out one thing about you—you'd give away your last cent to get attention, to feel like you're someone's first priority. If he makes you think he loves you, you'd give him the prizes, wouldn't you?"

"I—I wouldn't give him all of them…."

"Just most of them. Then he'll break your heart, baby."

"Oh. I—I've been making a fool of myself, haven't I?" she whispered. "He doesn't want me. He's been seducing me out of the prizes." She sounded sick now—as sick as Ben felt. Damn Hugh, knowing how to deliver a low blow! But he couldn't interfere; this had to be her choice, her decision. *Lucy, why can't you believe in yourself, or that I could fall head over heels in love with you?*

Because I never told her anything about myself, or the Capriati Curse!

He strode out. Yes, it had to be Lucy's decision—but it had to be based on the whole truth, and nothing but the truth. "Nice one, Dr. Carmody. Nice to see you care so much for Lucy, you'd tear her dreams and self-confidence apart to get what you want." He stood in front of his rival, arms folded, waiting.

It was obvious Monkey-boy had never been analyzed before. He flushed under his healthy bronze; his mouth opened and closed. "Hasn't anyone told you you shouldn't listen in on other people's conversations?" he snapped. "And her name's Abigail."

He faced Hugh squarely, not giving an inch. "Her name is

what *she* wants it to be, wouldn't you agree? Or are you such a control freak you can't even let her choose her own name?"

Lucy blinked, once, twice. "You're right, Ben." She turned to face Hugh, waiting for the answer. "Well?"

On the defensive, Hugh said, "Answer my question first! How long are you planning to be with poor Abigail before you dump her?"

"Actually, I don't want Abigail, poor or rich," Ben said mildly. "It's *Lucy* I want to be with—and for how long is as much up to her as me. She has as much a say in that as I do."

Lucy's lashes fluttered again; life and defiance flared in her lovely eyes. "Yeah, I do! What about that? You never thought of that, did you, Hugh? You never thought he might like me, but I could walk out on him, did you?"

Her sudden militancy left Dr. Dolittle floundering. "I—I…"

Then, as fast as it came, the brief burst of defiance faded; she only looked tired. "Just go now, Hugh, while we can still speak nicely to each other. It's over between us. Whether Ben hurts me or not is none of your business anymore."

Hugh stiffened. "I came all the way here for you. Don't I deserve some sort of—" he skidded to a halt, then added "—consideration?"

Lucy saw straight through it, as Ben did. "Don't you mean remuneration? If I had any money I'd offer it to you, Hugh, if only out of respect for what we used to be."

Ben, feeling her pain, said quietly, "If I offered you twenty thousand dollars to leave now, would you do it?"

"Make it thirty," Hugh replied, his eyes on fire with eagerness. "I could get another hundred scents for that!"

Ben glanced at Lucy, but to his amazement she seemed unsurprised by Hugh's skid-marks-left-on-the-floor defection. "Neither of us are giving you anything. Just get out of here, before we call the police for trespassing."

"If you think I'm leaving with nothing for my trouble—"
The heated words skidded to a halt as Ben advanced on him,
fists doubled. "Right. I think I'll—"

A sudden ear-piercing series of shrieks came from outside.

Hugh cried, "Oh, no," and he flew out the door, followed by
Lucy and Ben, where they found him petting and soothing—

"Your *monkeys?* You brought your *monkeys* with you to try
to get Lucy back?" Ben demanded, stunned by the other man's
sheer gall. "What the hell are you on—a scientific *Any Which
Way But Loose* road trip?"

He heard Lucy choke on laughter.

Hugh looked down his Roman nose as he carried the long,
extended cage inside the house to the kitchen floor. "Of course
I brought my experimental subjects. They can't be left alone.
Abigail understands the vital aspects of my research. She respects my work must come first at this stage."

"Actually, I don't," Lucy said pleasantly. "Get those smelly
animals out of my house and off my clean floors."

"*Your house?* You mean it's all sorted out and you won?"
Hugh gasped, a smile breaking out all over his face. "Oh,
snooky, that's great! We can sell everything to fund my research, and any left over from the sale we can keep for future
experiments—"

Lucy stepped back, folding her arms. "Um, you seem to
have forgotten—we broke up. Permanently. That hasn't
changed for me, even if it has for you since you suddenly think
I'm worth something."

Monkey-boy obviously recognized his danger; he gazed at
her, his handsome face boyish and pleading. "I always loved
you—but snooky, the money's important to both of us. You
know it means our future—"

"We don't have a future. And don't call me snooky. It's patronizing. Like being called Abigail when my name's Lucy."

Ben watched the jackass backpedal, finally realizing he had a fight on his hands to win Lucy—or the money—back. "Darling, of *course* it's your money, and I have no right to make plans with it. But I know how generous you are, how dedicated to science—"

"Dedicated, schmedicated," Lucy shot back. "I didn't know anything else but science until I came here! As for your research, not one cent of my money will go on it! I'm sick to death of your monkeys and their sexual reactions to scent!"

Hugh gaped at her. "Abigail! That is highly confidential!"

Ben gasped, "Um, Lucy, what exactly is Hugh researching?"

"Abigail, if you dare—!"

Lucy ignored the warning. "He's trying to make She-agra— a female version of Viagra," she announced in a tired voice.

Total silence for a moment, as he absorbed her words. Then he burst out laughing. "This is his *vital* experiment for humanity?" He doubled over, falling down the wall of the dining room. "Oh, man, oh, man—inadequate lovers of the world, unite!"

Lucy gasped, choked and laughed right with him. "I hadn't thought about it that way before…" She grinned up at Hugh.

Hugh looked livid. "This is *not* my vital research for humanity and you know it! This is getting corporate sponsorship for the research I really want. All scientists have to pay their dues. And for your information—" he glared at Ben "—many women happen to need this research. Many women would like to be able to enjoy normal marital intimacy—"

Slowly, Ben slid right down the wall to the floor, his gut aching—but he was no longer laughing. "Oh, man, how pathetic and arrogant science has become. How can you think you can fix the private lives of women you've never met?"

Lucy sat beside him, wiped her streaming eyes and grinned. "And did you get *your* knowledge of what women want from your occasional scientific journal?"

He grinned back. "Don't talk grown-up stuff with the children around," he murmured, pointing at the monkeys. He added softly, "Lucy, I'd rather sign away all the prizes to you now than have you believe I've just been vamping you this past week—and I will, if that's what it takes for you to believe me." She turned to look at him, unblinking. He looked right back into her eyes. "I've always known you might be vamping me, too—but it's a chance I'm willing to take, if it means being with you."

After a long, tense moment, she shook herself, and slipped her hand into his. "This has been a confusing day."

He squeezed her hand, feeling so peaceful, so *right* sitting on the floor, just holding her hand. "Is it over with him, Lucy?"

She gave him a watery smile. "What do you think? But I feel really overloaded right now. My life is changing in front of my eyes, and I need time to come to terms with that."

"I'll wait," he whispered.

"Abigail, come home. Your parents are expecting you," Hugh barked—and he actually had the gall to snap his fingers at her.

Lucy snapped back without missing a beat, "Oh, bite me, Monkey-boy—and take your gorillas into the mist with you! Ben and I have dinner waiting."

"And you're going to risk that he's—"

She smiled at her ex-fiancé. "You know what you never even considered, Hugh? That just because you're not interested in me, doesn't mean Ben isn't."

"Come on, Abigail! You seriously think *you* can seduce *him?*"

At that, Ben lost what remained of his patience. "Oh, take a hike, Dr. Dolittle," he snarled. "Take your stinky best friends and leave Lucy and me to our mutual vamping attempts. The sooner you go, the sooner we find out who won and you can try to wangle more scents for your little mates in the cages."

"If you think I'm leaving Abigail to be seduced out of—"

"Oh, just go, Hugh, or I'll leave the prizes to Ben!" Lucy snapped. "The way I feel about you, I'd rather Ben had them all!"

Silence greeted this ultimatum. Within a minute, the front door slammed shut, leaving Ben and Lucy alone.

Lucy sighed, laying her head on his shoulder.

"You okay?" he asked softly.

She looked up, saw Hugh was gone and nodded. "Of all the arrogant—that'll teach him to think he can snap his fingers at me and walk off with all my prizes!"

Songs were sung about it. Books and poems were written about it. His sister Sofie had cried on his shoulder about it. But he'd never been able to imagine what a broken heart felt like until this minute. It hurt even to breathe. Damn it, after all he'd done to make her look at him, *really* look at him, was he just a means to her original end? Did she still love that creep?

"Yeah." His voice was scratchy. "That'll teach him."

How on earth could he get this delicious armful of woman to know he was head over feet in love with her, without scaring her into bolting back to her old, safe life?

He couldn't fight it, or deny it. He'd followed the best and most terrifying of the Capriati traditions: he'd fallen madly in love with Lucy, his total opposite, within a day—a woman who thought he was a beach-bum dropout, a man she probably wouldn't consider keeping in her life for longer than the week they'd planned, if Monkey-boy hadn't fueled her anger. He'd had to fight every preconceived notion she had of him, this past week, just to gain a little of her respect, let alone anything else.

But for him, every moment with Lucy only left him more in love with her, chained to the hope that if he hung around long enough, did enough for her, she'd see him as a real man, and worthy of her love.

And he knew that if she left him, he'd mourn her loss the rest of his life. Like Uncle Enzo when Aunt Katarina died, and Uncle Giuseppe when Aunt Anna ran off for six months to become an actress.

And he'd grinned and joked about it behind his back, like the rest of the kids. He didn't laugh now. All he knew was he had to take a chance with Lucy now, for better or—*gulp*—for worse. He had to tell her the truth about himself…all of it, from being a doctor and deceiving her about it, to the fact that he was crazy in love with her, or he could lose her forever.

"Lucy, I have to tell you something—"

A rumble of a truck's wheels came, down the street, heavy and lumbering, and slowly came to a stop outside the house.

Ben's radar for potential embarrassment went onto high alert even before the truck's doors slammed again—and he heard voices he recognized, with a sinking heart.

Well, he'd been expecting them for the past week, hadn't he? Now here they were, and of course they'd turned up with all their usual worst possible timing. It was a Curse thing; it had to be. No witch's calling down on him could wreak more havoc than this lot with just a few words.

Mama's warm, musical voice filled the air with her weary anger. "I don't care if I've said it all the way from Sydney, Franco—this is still an invasion of his privacy!"

"Are you saying our Benny wouldn't welcome us to his home, Gloria?" Papa demanded, his deep, gruff backstreets-of-Sydney-meets-New-Jersey voice overrode Mama's with ease by its unique accent.

Ben sighed and covered his eyes with a hand. "It had to be now, didn't it? Right after Tarzan swings out, they swing in…."

Lucy touched his arm. "Who is it, Ben?" she whispered.

"It's a nice place, Vincenzo," *Nonna's* voice, thick with nasal Italian-American twang remarked, through huffing and puffing. "Benny's done real good for himself. It's a nice place for a vacation. Sun, sand, the warmth, right on the water…"

Now in total despair—for as much as he loved his grandparents, they were walking disasters as far as his love life had always been concerned—Ben muttered, "Did they have to come, too? We'll never get rid of them now!"

"Ben?" Lucy faltered, looking worried. "What's the matter?"

"Benny?" A thunderous knock made the door shudder. "Benny, you home?"

"The jig's up." Ben groaned and got to his feet. "I knew it was too good to last. I knew they'd find me, sooner or later."

"But who is it?" she whispered, as rowdy banging started on the front door.

He sighed. It was all over now. Any chance he had with Lucy was gone the moment he opened the door to his loving, noisy, overpowering relatives, and they saw her. "It's my family."

Chapter Twelve

Lucy had no time to absorb the information before Ben opened the door, and a riot of people exploded into the house.

"Ben, darling!" A nicely rounded, middle-aged woman hugged and kissed him, wearing a smile that could light up a room—Ben's smile. "I'm sorry. When the reporter from the paper called about interviewing us about your win, we found out where you were. I tried to stop them...."

"I know, Mama," Ben said, sounding depressed, hugging her.

A burly, middle-aged man with the same lush, earthy good looks as Ben, demanded, "Why should you stop us seeing Benny, Gloria?" He spoke in an Italian-American-meets-Sydney-backstreets accent that was sort of cute. "Isn't he my firstborn son? Can't I come to my own son's house if I want to?" He, too, hugged Ben. "You okay, boy?" His gruff tone couldn't conceal the intense love this man held for his son.

With a twitching grin, Ben hugged his father back. "I'm fine, Papa. I've just been having a holiday, that's all."

"You needed it, too. Five years without a break. You're gonna work yourself into an early grave one of these days. You need a wife to look after you."

"Not now, Papa, okay?" Ben sounded edgy. He flicked a glance at Lucy, nervous, unsure.

"Nice place, Benny-boy. I can see myself here, lazing in the sun, checkin' out the chicky-babes...." A chubby, cherubic old man with a strong Bronx-Italian accent caught sight of Lucy, standing behind Ben, not sure what to make of this sudden cacophony of light and sound. "Ah-ha! No wonder he didn't tell us about the house, Stefani! He's got himself shacked up with a chicky-babe. And a pretty little gal to boot. Ah, Benny-boy, you're a man after your old *Nonno's* heart!"

The thin, birdlike old lady beside the man kissed Ben, then peered at Lucy. "Hmm...not his usual type—no dyed hair, no war paint, no implants—and she actually looks like she's got some brains. Maybe this is The One! I hope so. I like her better than your usual bimbos," she pronounced with a gap-toothed grin. "She don't hang all her wares out in the store window, know what I'm sayin'? What's her name?"

The One? Shacked up? *Implants?* Not used to this type of rapid dissection, Lucy blinked and tried to speak, but her mouth wouldn't work.

Ben's father demanded, "And, more importantly, if you are The One, are you a Catholic?"

Ben took Lucy's hand. "Stop it, Papa. She doesn't have to put up with the third degree in her own house!"

Everyone gasped. "*Her* house? Did you *marry* her, Benny? Without us to be here to give you a blessing?" his father roared.

"Did you marry her in the church?" the old man asked avidly.

"He'd better have, Papa, or we don't recognize their babies!" Ben's father snapped.

"She could make the change," Ben's grandmother suggested, checking Lucy out for signs of potential Capriati offspring. "I'll talk to Father Bonatti. I *like* this one!"

"I won't have my grandchildren becoming the first Capriatis buried outside consecrated ground, Benny, you hear me?"

"I'd say half of Queensland heard you, Papa," Ben said dryly. "Is it any use telling you there's no chance of more Capriati babies at this stage?"

Ben's small, birdlike grandmother pinched her son's arm. "Don't alienate Benny, Franco...listen to your mother!"

"All of you, stop it!" Ben's mother elbowed her husband in turn. "We don't even know the girl's name yet!"

Everyone stopped again. As one they turned to Lucy, who, overwhelmed, shrank behind Ben.

"Can someone please tell me the chicky-babe's name?" Ben's grandfather asked mildly.

"Lucy!" Lucy cried, her hands over her ears. "I'm Lucy Miles, I'm Irish-Australian and I'm scientific, not religious!"

Dead silence.

"You're not religious?" Ben's father spoke in a quiet that was more stunning than his previous roars. "Not even a nominal religion? What are your parents?"

"They're s-scientists." The stutter of embarrassment amazed her. Was she actually *apologizing* for her brilliant parents?

"But what religion were they christened into?" Franco asked impatiently. "They had to be christened. Everyone was back then!"

Lucy thought about it. "I—I think my grandparents were Catholic...they came out from Dublin on the same boat. It's how my parents met, when they were children. And I do believe in God. I've never been part of any organized religion, that's all," Lucy explained earnestly.

"Well, that's something," Ben's father said cheerfully. "Good girl. We didn't want Benny hooked up with the wrong kind, that's all."

Lucy shrank right away. "We didn't hook up! I've only been here a week. We're just waiting to see who won the sweepstakes."

More silence. Everyone stared at her, then at Ben.

"There was a mix-up at the lottery office," he said, shrugging. "She has a right to be here."

"I discovered that I hold an identical ticket to Ben's, the one that won the sweepstakes. They're working out which of us won the prizes." Lucy cringed, waiting for the axe to fall.

The smiles aimed her way faded. "You wanna take Benny's prizes?" Franco Capriati asked, sounding stunned.

Ben's grandmother said reasonably, "Why wouldn't she? Can't blame her if she got the same ticket. We'd be cheerin' Benny on if it was him."

"Thank you," Lucy gasped in relief. She smiled tentatively at Ben's grandmother, who smiled back, her dark eyes twinkling. Just like Ben's. "I don't want everything, I really don't. Just my share."

Ben's *Nonna* beamed. "Good girl. You're not greedy. I like that." She came to her and patted her cheek, in a gentle, maternal gesture Lucy had never known. "You like my Benny? He's a good boy. You might wanna think about marryin' him. He's a real good catch."

Ben gulped so hard Lucy felt it. "*Nonna,* can you please let me handle my own love life?"

The old lady gave her gap-toothed grin again. "Benny, you're thirty-one, darlin'. It's past time to settle down. And this one's the first nice girl you've had since Letizia Venuti, when you were sixteen. And you like this girl a lot. I can see you do. Is this the—"

"*Nonna,* will you please let me work this out?" Ben sounded almost despairing now. "I need to talk to Lucy myself."

Then *Nonna's* eyebrows lifted. "Aha!" Her eyes lit. "So it's true—it finally happened to you, *mi bambino?*"

Vincenzo grinned. "Ah, the Capriati Curse. About time it finally hit you, Benny." Vincenzo patted Ben's shoulder. "You know how it works—it comes late, but it comes hard. You're a goner now. You ain't gonna change girls for anyone."

Nonna said, nodding in satisfaction, "Now I don't have to worry he'll have babies comin' into the world with dye bottles and silicon bags in their hands. Nice girl, nice babies. I'm proud of you, Benny."

Every word Ben's family spoke left Lucy in deeper confusion. "W-what's the Capriati Curse?"

Ben's hand jerked in hers. His mother looked at Lucy, and sighed quietly. "Oh, dear."

The rest of the family all stopped and stared at her for a moment. Ben's grandfather chuckled, and cuddled his wife. "It's the bane of all Capriati men, *cara.* But there's no gettin' round it. If Benny's got it with you—and he sure looks like it, the way he's lookin' at you—he's got no choice but to marry you. So, welcome to the family!" He beamed at her.

Lucy felt the color drain from her cheeks. Pushed into early-learning centers and elite schools, given little choice but to become a librarian—even her relationship with Hugh had been orchestrated, and their relationship had been defined by whatever he wanted from her. Now, just when she'd begun to feel that she'd met a man who respected her enough to let her control her life, these people were taking away her fledgling confidence.

So she'd run away from home, and the reputation of being a nuisance, only to come here and be upgraded to a full-blown— "I'm a *Curse* to you?" she whispered to Ben, trying hard not to cry.

Panic flared in his eyes. "No, Lucy—you don't understand. It's true I had no choice in this—it's like a destiny thing—but—" He grabbed her hands in his. "I can't talk about this in front of everyone. Can we go somewhere?"

She shook her head. "Not now. Um, excuse me," she said to his family, her voice faint. "I'll leave you to enjoy your visit with Ben. I—I need to get a few things down the road."

His face pale, he said quietly, "I'll come with you."

"No, thanks." She shook her head. "I...need time to think."

"He's a real good catch, honey," *Nonna* sounded anxious now. "You know it's always real handy to have a husband who's a—"

"*Nonna!* Please, let me tell her!" Ben interrupted sharply. He tipped up Lucy's chin, gazing into her eyes. "Please let me come with you? We need to talk."

Lucy broke away from his arms. "I need to take a d-drive. By myself."

Without any further argument, he reached into his pocket. "Take the convertible. It's safer. I'll worry about you in that car of yours. It's ready for the scrap heap."

She bit her lip. "But, you see, it's mine," she whispered. "It might be the only thing I have to own or control in my life, but it's all mine."

"Okay." He shoved the keys back in his jeans, and led her to the hall stand where her bag, cardigan and keys hung. "We have to talk, Lucy. I need to tell you things you don't know."

She gave him a watery smile. "Obviously. I just don't know if I'm ready to hear it now. I kinda feel overloaded." She said softly, for him alone, "I need to make sense of all this. I can't do that with so many people around. I'm used to doing everything on my own. To being on my own."

His eyes searched hers, with uncomfortable depth. "All right, Lucy. I can wait until you're ready." He caressed her face with the tenderness that had become her lifeline the past week, her anchor and rock in a shifting world. "I won't change the locks while you're gone. Trust me."

"I know you wouldn't," she whispered. "Thank you." Helpless in her turbulent confusion, she turned and walked out the door.

Ben turned from watching her leave, to see four pairs of eyes watching him in identical depth of concern. "Don't say it—any of you," he growled.

"How long did it take, Benny?" Papa asked.

"Half an hour, all right?" He shoved a hand through his hair. "Okay, you can all start laughing. I swore it would never happen to me, and it did."

"What's the fight, son?" his papa asked quietly, putting a comforting hand on his shoulder.

He rubbed his forehead, feeling a dull throb start behind his eyes. "Her fiancé dumped her five days ago. He came here today. She knows he doesn't love her, that he only wants the money, but her family approves of her relationship with him, and that's important to her. He comes from her world—the only world she's ever known. She likes me, but she's not ready to look at my feelings for her. She doesn't trust me." He sighed again. "It's my fault. I haven't told her anything about myself. I didn't want it to be like it's been with the others. I wanted her to like *me*, not what I do or what I earn. I played a beach-bum playboy in the beginning—trying to deny it was the Curse—and now she believes that's all I am. I have to change that."

Franco smiled adoringly at his wife, sharing a memory thirty-three years old. He'd tried so hard to impress her with his wit and smile, not even knowing he could never top the way he'd broken up with his fiancée for the sake of loving her at first sight. But still, he'd had to fight through Gloria's loyalty to her friend who had been Franco's fiancée, and the fear that he was a playboy who'd walk out on her as he had on Cecilia.

Ben saw the look, and ached for the repeating of a history he'd never wanted…but he couldn't imagine not meeting Lucy, even if he lost her forever and had to give her all the prizes. Not knowing Lucy, never loving her, was unthinkable.

Nonna came to Ben, hugging him with all the strength her tiny frame belied. "We're here for you, *bambino*. We'll help you get your little gal."

He closed his eyes. Much as he loved his family, five minutes in their company had all but driven Lucy out the door. "Thanks, *Nonna*, but I think I should handle this myself." He turned and walked up the stairs on feet that felt lead lined. Damn it, this part of it really was a Curse….

"We've got to help Benny," *Nonna* reiterated when Ben had gone.

Gloria stared narrow eyed at her mother-in-law. "What makes you think he needs our help, Mama?"

Nonna rolled her eyes. "Why do you think, Gloria? The little gal's a sweetheart, but she's Irish."

Gloria rolled her eyes but didn't speak. Her mother-in-law loved her dearly, but still hadn't forgiven her for her Irish descent. It would be nice to have an ally in the family for once.

"So what have you got in mind, darlin'?" Vincenzo asked his wife, beaming at her. "Nobody hatches up better plans than you."

"I don't want to know!" Gloria Capriati walked to the door. "Since it seems we aren't going to leave Ben to work out his own life, I'm going to buy the groceries that, knowing my oldest son who looks after everyone but himself, he hasn't bothered to get!" She sighed and jerked the door open—then jumped back into her husband's arms, screaming.

A glorious young man, like a blond Greek god, bent over a cage with about seven chimpanzees in it, looked up and screamed right back at her.

Chapter Thirteen

Lucy sat at a bench at a quiet inlet, her hands between her knees, looking out over the water, searching for answers to questions she didn't even want to ask herself, let alone Ben.

Was she just a curse to him?

Did he really care about her, or was Hugh right—was he vamping her to get the advantage with the sweepstakes?

The question is, does it matter whether he likes you or is vamping you? Either way, you've been having fun! So why cry about it now? Watch out, Lucy girl, this could be love...

"No!" she muttered, jerking her cardigan down over her arms as the air cooled with evening. "I'm not falling for Ben—I want a man like Hugh, who wants the same things in life as I do."

Like the wedding? Yeah, Hugh really seemed to want that!

"Like attracts like, and Ben and I are nothing alike!"

But opposites also attract in science, and the bond is stronger...look at positive and negative ions. A fusion of opposite compounds can only be separated by catalystic force,

or they remain together eternally. Most similarly forced mol-
ecules can only be bonded by an opposite force ion. Classic
example: water.

She groaned. "It's not going to happen! Fun and games for
one week only! That's all it is with Ben, and all it ever will
be! I will not be any man's curse—ever!"

"Abigail?"

Startled yet resigned, having half expected his interruption
in her life again at some stage, she swiveled around in the seat.
"It's over, Hugh."

Hugh stood behind her, his golden, handsome face as glorious as ever, yet it left her cold. "I haven't come to nag you."

"Then what is it?"

He sighed, and held out a plain white envelope. "There's
something you need to know before you make any decisions
about your life. Something I've been keeping from you the
past two years."

"Benny?" A knock came at his bedroom door. Papa's voice,
anxious and loving, told him there was no way he'd get away
with pretending to be asleep.

He rolled over on the bed, pulling pillows behind his head.
"Come in."

Mama was with him. "Would you like to talk about it, darling?" she asked softly.

He shrugged. "Her boyfriend called it a shipboard romance. He could see the mistakes I've made with her after ten
minutes. I've spent the whole week giving her the fun she's
never had, I've shown her how much I care, but I haven't told
her the truth about who and what I am—even though I know
all about her. I can't blame her for her lack of faith."

Mama shook her head, smiling. "Silly boy. You spend years
learning about people, and still you know so little. You find

out all about her life, her work, her relationships, hopes and fears, and you didn't know to give the same trust back to her? If she's been totally honest with you, sweetheart, and you've only given her fun and games so far, on what can she base that trust a woman must have to give a man her heart? What *does* she know about you?"

"Nothing but the family," he groaned, feeling like a complete jerk. "I mean, she knows *me*—"

"But not the things that make a woman feel secure." Papa sat beside him on the bed. "If there's anything I learned from wooing your mama, son, it's this—if you want to be real to a woman, you have to *give* her reality. Tell her who you are, what you do, about your hopes and dreams and fears. Otherwise, you're no more real to her than the shipboard romance the Monkey-man called you. And it looks to me like this girl don't take to shocks too well, Benny. Tell her everything about yourself she doesn't know, including the Curse, before someone else does by accident."

"The Monkey-man?" he asked sharply. "How did you—"

Papa grinned. "He's been and gone, son. And somehow I don't think he's coming back."

He gave his parents a watery smile. "God bless family."

Papa hugged him, rough and tender. "You been doing things on your own too long, boy. Two jobs and school, and then working all those ungodly hours, not letting us help you. It's our turn now." He grinned. "We've all been through the Curse, Benny. Don't throw away the help we can give you, just to be independent."

Without warning, he felt all choked up. "Thanks, Papa."

"You love her that much, son?" Mama touched his shoulder.

Simply, he nodded. "She stormed into the house and straight into my heart. She's the other half of me now. I can't imagine my life without her."

"Then go get her, boy." Papa slapped his arm. "Trust me. She wanted space, you respected her wish…but you give her too much time, and she'll think you don't care enough to chase her. If she's ever going to love you, she needs to *feel* your love, son. And she needs your truth. All of it."

A single glance at Mama's nod sent him to his feet. "Thanks, guys." He hugged and kissed them both. "As I said before. God bless family!"

An hour later, still roaring around the Gold Coast streets on Jan, he finally found her.

It looked as though she'd been on the park bench for a while. She was shivering beneath her cardigan—the wind was cool tonight—and her hair was in a wild tangle. There was an open envelope in her hand, and a letter spread across her knees, held down with a firm hand. Her face was pale, yet resolute.

Something inside that determination got his heart thudding and his gut in all kinds of knots. "Lucy?"

"I thought it was you. I heard the bike." She didn't turn around, didn't move. "I've been gone a long time, haven't I? Sorry if I worried you."

"It's okay. I just hated the thought of you alone in the dark, and I worried that the car might have broken down." He approached her cautiously. "I brought you a hamburger. I thought you might be hungry. Can I sit down?"

"Yes, you know that about me, all right. I'm always hungry." Her face warmed with a little, sweet half smile as she took the brown paper bag from him, pulled out the just-warm burger and ate with all her usual gusto.

"Is it still a bad time? I'll go again if you want to be alone." He sat beside her, glad he'd brought a spare jacket. He laid it across her shoulders. "You look cold."

"I am. Oh, this is much better," she sighed, digging into the simple burger, and snuggling into the jacket with a smile. She didn't speak again until she'd finished her food, and cleaned her hands. "Don't go, Ben. We both have things we need to say."

Why that terrified him, he didn't know…but with a clarity he'd give anything not to have, he knew, somehow, that he was going to lose her. "You want to talk first?"

The letter on her lap crackled as she folded it, and held it inside her fist. "I'd rather hear yours first."

He nodded. Dragging in a deep breath, he said quietly, "The first and most important thing you need to know is that I love you, Lucy. I think I've loved you from the first day we met."

She gasped softly, but didn't speak, didn't move, either to him or away. Waiting.

"You wanted to know what the Capriati Curse is." He shoved his cold, trembling hands inside his leather jacket. "It's been around for over a hundred and fifty years now. My great-great-grandfather was apparently quite a lad with the ladies. He made the mistake of fooling around with the daughter of the local wisewoman, without serious intentions. He broke the girl's heart—and her mother cursed him and all his male descendants, that we'd all fall in love in a day with a woman who's our exact opposite, and we'd learn how it felt to have to fight for love. And he did. He fell for this quiet, serious girl who made him wait seven years while she nursed her mother…but he didn't mind waiting for her, apparently. His wandering days were over."

He shrugged, feeling like a total dork admitting it. "But I didn't want to believe in it, even though I'd seen its effects on my family all my life. I didn't want to admit some stupid curse had any control over my life…and I couldn't stand the idea of being like the rest of the men in my family, so in love they'd do anything, make any sacrifice to be with the woman they

oved." He watched her curls tossing around in the breeze, and
smiled. "Then I met you, and before long I knew it happened
to me, just like it had to the rest of my family."

Her continued silence, the tiny frown between her eyebrows unnerved him. "I know, the whole idea of the men in
our family being cursed sounds stupid. But it happened to
Nonno with *Nonna*. She joined the USO during the war. He
was about to be shipped to France. He saw her as he was
boarding the boat, and proposed on the spot. She thought he
was nuts. Every time he got leave he searched all over En-
gland, until he found her. He couldn't let go."

She turned to him, and smiled. "And your parents?"

He gulped. "Papa saw Mama at his wedding rehearsal to
another woman. She was his bride's bridesmaid. He broke up
with the girl, and four months later, Mama and Papa got married—and thirty-two years later, they're still crazy in love."

"So, is this really a curse?" she asked, sounding puzzled.
"Sounds like it brings a lot of happiness to the Capriati men.
Your father and grandfather seem to love their wives dearly."

His head spun. "I never thought of that. Yes, you're right.
They're all incredibly happy." He grinned at her. "Maybe it
should be called the Capriati Blessing from now on."

Her eyebrows lifted. "Well, I'd certainly prefer to be part
of a blessing than a curse. I'm kind of tired of always being
seen as a negative in people's lives."

"So you believe me?" he asked slowly.

"I—yes." She let out a breath. "Your grandmother said
you're a good catch? Your Papa said you're working yourself
to death. I guess that means that, unless being a beach bum is
a lot harder and pays better than I thought, that you have a job?"

"Yes, I do." Man, this was so *hard*. "I never meant to de-
ceive you about it."

She went totally still at those words. "But you did?"

The words, filled with such gentle pain, stabbed him to the heart. "Yes," he mumbled. "Do you remember I told you I endured years of university?"

She nodded, not looking at him.

"I inferred I was a dropout. Actually, I had a working scholarship. I worked my way through four years, then two years of medical school before I gained my internship and three years residency. I just finished last month."

"You're a doctor." It wasn't a question.

Ben gave a tiny sigh. "Yeah."

She nodded. "That makes sense. I thought you'd probably studied something scientific. You knew about palaeontology, land salinity and how to check my leg for breaks." With a shrug, she gave a laugh that held no mirth or music. "My fault, really, isn't it? I didn't ask. I didn't want to know." She flushed. "You must have thought I was an idiot when I tried to help you find a job."

"No." He tilted her face up to gaze into her eyes. "I thought it was incredibly sweet of you."

She pulled away. "Don't patronize me, Ben. I'm not a child to be placated with a compliment."

"I'm not. You don't understand. Ever since I got my scholarship I've had girls, women, after me. 'This is Ben the doctor,' they'd say. Women liked me for what I did, not who I am. The fact that you tried to help me showed me you cared about *me,* not my job. It touched me. I should have told you then, but—" he smiled at her through his pain "—but you charmed me, Lucy. You thought I was a beach bum, and you liked me anyway. I didn't want to lose that feeling."

"You didn't trust me enough to be honest with me, did you?"

That was Lucy, straight to the soul of the matter, even if it hurt. He sighed again. "I guess not. I thought—I just wanted you to care for *me,* not Ben the doctor."

"I was honest with you from the start. I told you about my engagement, my hopes and dreams. About Hugh, and my family. I told you about the sweepstakes, why I wanted to win. I even told you how much I wanted you. I thought you were a nice guy, despite all you'd done to show me you were the opposite of what you really are. At least Hugh was honest when he ignored me...." She pressed her lips together, as if fighting tears. "Is this your idea of love, Ben?"

"No," he muttered, shame washing through him. "I'm sorry, Lucy. My only defense is that I did it when I didn't know you—and I didn't want to recognize that I was falling for you. I was even less honest with myself than with you. By the time I knew I loved you, I didn't know how to fix what I'd done without losing you." He closed his eyes. "I don't expect you to forgive me."

She kept looking out to the ocean, but a small smile was in her voice. "But you're hoping to disarm me with this sudden burst of honesty, aren't you? Trying to show me you're capable of it?"

A rumbling chuckle came from his gut. "You know me too well, don't you?" He turned to her. "But at least now you know what I meant when I said we have important things in common. We both work in science, and want to help people."

"You said you've finished your residency. What are you going to do now?"

The distance inside her words scared him. "About two months ago I signed a five-year contract to serve a series of country towns on the edge of Outback New South Wales, starting in January. They have the Flying Doctor to service their emergency needs, and they get a clinic every two months, but there are six thousand people in the region, including isolated farmers. They have two community nurses, but they need a doctor of their own, a hospital—even if it's a tiny one until I can organize another doctor to join me." He hesitated. "It will be an on-call job, with only Sundays off unless there's an emergency."

Without warning the wind picked up, roaring through with an unseasonal chill, the precursor of the spring storm called a Southerly Buster. She shivered and turned into him, seeking his warmth. Joy and terror sliced into him as he held her. Would this be the last time he ever had her in his arms? He didn't speak, didn't ask the question. She had a lot to think through.

Eventually she stirred against him. "It sounds like a hard life, but a rewarding one."

"I know. Somehow it didn't feel right to be a city doctor. I wanted to go where I'd be needed." He took in a slow breath, cleansing his lungs, praying for courage. "Could you handle that kind of life?"

She pulled back to gaze at him. "What are you asking, Ben?"

For answer, he took her hand and pulled off the plastic ring. "I want to put another ring there," he muttered, in a low voice. "A fire opal as vivid and beautiful and mercurial as you are. If you can forgive me, I want you with me for the rest of my life. I love you, Lucy—more than you could imagine. Will you marry me?"

In the half-dreaming light of oncoming dusk, he waited for the words that would decide his life, his destiny.

But her words were neither what he'd hoped, nor feared. "Hugh found me before you did," she said softly. "Today, I mean. He had a secret confession, too."

"The letter?" His voice sounded strangled with fear. This meant too much. *She* meant too much.

"Yes." She pulled away from him, her head lowered. "It was from Professor Langtree, the director of rural experiments at Brandt University. Two years ago, he invited me to submit the data for my experiment on apple growing, and he offered me a grant for a year's research." She sighed. "Hugh got to the letter first. He wrote back to Professor Langtree as me, saying I'd found funding elsewhere."

Yeah, and he knew why. "Selfish jerk didn't want you to steal his thunder."

"Yes—and he didn't want to lose his meek, supportive little worshipper. If I had my own glory, I might find I didn't need him…and he might lose Mother and Father's clout with the university to give financial support for his She-agra project."

Ben frowned. "So why give it to you now?"

"I wish I knew." She shrugged helplessly. "He called Professor Langtree and told him what he'd done." Her fingers fiddled with the paper, making it rustle. "I've been offered the same research grant for one year. Starting in six weeks."

His body jerked in shock. "That's when my tenure starts." And then he knew her answer. "This is your dream come true."

"I know." Her voice shook. "I don't know why Hugh did this for me, but—"

"But you can't let it pass. You have to take it."

She turned to him, her eyes wild, her hair swirling around her sweet face. "I think I should leave in the morning, no matter who wins the sweepstakes. Ben—"

"I know, Lucy. I understand." He took her cold face in his hands and kissed her, and when she kissed him back, he knew he wasn't the only one to feel too much, want too much; they were both shaking. "You have to go. I can't ask you to turn your back on your dream for mine. We'll split the prizes. I want you to have enough money to look after yourself."

"Thank you." The wind tossed her hair across her face. The first raindrop fell, landing on her cheek, falling like a tear. "I—I think I could have fallen in love with you, Ben."

The finality touched his soul. "But you didn't."

"Give me time," she said softly. "It's too soon since my engagement to Hugh. So much has happened this week, and you have a lot of honesty to catch up on. I need to see that you *are* the nice guy I thought you were before confession time. I'm not someone who can make a fast one-eighty—not without evidence that my life and heart will be safe with you." Her eyes twinkled with gentle self-mockery. "We can get to know each other better. We can write, or call. If—if you'll wait—"

He gave her a wry smile in the gathering darkness. "The term 'once and forever' takes on a whole new definition in our family, Lucy. We wait. We Capriati men don't get a lot of choice in the matter."

She smiled at him then. "I like that idea."

He kissed her palm. "It's raining, and neither of us can afford to get sick. Let's go home." He walked her to her old car. He opened the driver's door for her. "I want you to take the convertible when you go. Will you do that for me? I'll worry about your safety in this car."

She gave him a lilting smile. "Hey, buster, that car could still be mine."

He no longer cared whose prizes they were—there was only one prize he wanted. She could take the whole lot now, so long as she took him with them. "Then you'll take it?"

"Yes—but only under strong protest." She gave him another glimmering smile. "The sacrifices I make for you, Capriati."

How was he going to let her go? He needed her so badly, his little Irish dreamer who'd snuggled into his heart as if she'd always belonged there. She could even make him smile when he was losing her. "I'll see you at home. One of *Nonna's* fabulous linguines is waiting for us."

He followed her car toward home, wondering if this was déjà vu to come—always watching Lucy leave, but loving her anyway.

* * *

After a raging storm that night, the next morning dawned clear and dewy bright. The convertible held a new suitcase in it, one Ben had given her, filled with her things. She had the TV and DVD player, and a few kitchen appliances. That was all she'd agreed to take. "It's more than I expected when I came," she said softly. "I don't need any more than this, Ben. I'll be too busy to be home much, anyway."

The gentle caring in her tone, considering his feelings, made his heart overflow with love. "I'll send you half the house sale price."

They'd already relinquished their claims to further prizes or compensation from Lakelands Children's Charity. Mr. Hill and the board had been grovelingly grateful for their generosity—and for their discretion. They'd sent a brief statement of their decision to the media last night, refusing to sell their story for cash, despite lucrative offers.

She shook her head. "Keep it, just in case. If—" She bit her lip.

"I'll send it to you if you need it. Just ask." His voice was gruff.

She nodded, her eyes misty. "I'd better go." She smiled uncertainly at his family, still hovering near the doorway. "Bye. I hope I meet you all again." The Capriatis waved, and, with understanding smiles, vanished inside the house.

He watched her, aching, unsure. And though it was broad daylight and the neighbors could see them, she gave a tiny cry and flung herself into his arms. Their kiss was long, hard and almost desperate. "I'm scared, Ben," she whispered.

He held her against his thumping heart, wishing he didn't have to say the words. It grated through his throat, hurting him, but he said it for her sake. "You'll be fine. Your experiment will be a big success. A triumph for science."

She looked up at him. "You think so?"

"I know it. You're going to make it, Lucy. And remember, I'm only a phone call away if you need someone in your corner."

Her glimmering smile came to life. "That's one thing I do know." She kissed him again. "You've been—such a good friend to me. I'll miss you."

"Me, too. From the minute you go." He held her hard against him, and whispered into her ear, "Make time to dance, Lucy. Make time for sunrises and sunsets, and maybe a little sand surfing."

"I will," she whispered back. "I promise."

He couldn't control the words. "Just don't kiss any other dark strangers on the dance floor, all right?"

She smiled, and softly kissed his shoulder. "If I feel the need to play Marilyn, you'll be the first person I'll call."

Even hurting like hell, he chuckled. "I love you."

She pulled back to look into his eyes with a sweet tenderness that melted his heart and made him wish like crazy for another minute, another day—a lifetime of keeping that look in her eyes when she was with him.

Let her go. Don't say it...don't make her feel guilty for having the right to choose her own life...

She touched his face, trailing her fingers down his jaw. She blinked hard. "Bye, Ben. I—"

She bit her lip, turned and ran into the convertible, put it in gear and drove off without looking back.

Chapter Fourteen

Nine Months Later

'**D**r. Capriati, dear, here's another letter from your lady."

"Thanks." Ben looked up from the letter he was writing to Lucy. He smiled wearily at Marge Bright, one of a legion of women in town who refused to let him look after himself at home.

Monilough still held small-town status, and the people were so grateful he'd chosen to help them in the pretty, half-wild isolated Outback town, putting himself on seven-day call, they took care of him in almost every other way. That included getting him a wife, until he told them he was engaged—well, he was in his own heart. But though they'd given up on fixing his love life, they mowed his lawn, cooked and cleaned and threw thank-you parties—and he didn't have the heart to tell them that it only left him aching, hungering for—

He'd go to the parties, wishing he could smile with Lucy at a joke, dance with her to the boot-scootin' music they preferred here, hold her in his arms for the slow dances. But more than anything else, he wanted to have the right to take her home at night and make love to her, and wake up every morning in her arms.

He kept aside every day at dusk for writing to her. Even if he only managed half a page he sent it, along with cute cards and funny notes and pictures of the Outback. He told her about the time a very drunk Bert Cluff fell headfirst down a mine shaft, still attached to his ankle rope, suspended in mid-air for an hour, alternately screaming and snoring before anyone found him. He told her about Phil MacIntyre, who got four broken ribs and five days of amnesia after riding his unimpressed prize bull through town to get Jenny Simpkins to notice him. He told her the names of every baby he'd delivered, every child he immunized or stitched up, the kindness of the people in town. And he told her about a certain two-hundred acre patch of ground for sale, right beside the house he'd bought as a home-cum-surgery until the renovations on his offices in town were complete.

She wrote back almost every day, and called twice a week. Her experiment seemed to be going well. Results were steadily trickling in. She was putting in as many hours as he did, but she was always conscientious about taking time out for fun with her friends at the University Research Center. Her parents were cautious in their praise, but they'd said they were proud of her. Even Hugh couldn't believe the results she'd gained so fast.

He tried not to worry, but, though she wrote and called so often, and told him she missed him, she never said she loved him. And—surely some of the guys on campus saw Lucy's strong adorable factor, the vivid blue of her eyes, or the sweetness of her smile? And what was Hugh doing, still hanging around?

Yeah, Ben was fighting for her love, all right—he had to fight himself to give her the space to fly, to find the woman she wanted to be, the life she wanted. He would not be like Hugh or her parents, demanding she do—or become—what would make him happy. He loved her as she was, and respected her right to make the choice…but oh, the days and nights, empty and aching with the memory of her face, waiting, just waiting…

Then he read the words on the paper in his hand, and slowly, the black ink turned misty red before his eyes.

"Hugh proposed to me in front of Mother and Father today, and he actually said I'd proven myself worthy to be his wife! Can you believe it?"

Yeah, he believed it all right…and the red mists became a burst of fire in his brain. No way. No *way* would he let that—that *monkey lover* take his girl! Lucy wasn't a convenience for any man, especially one who needed her to be *worthy* of him.

He scrunched the letter to a tiny ball in his hand—like he'd love to do to Monkey-boy. This wasn't gonna happen! Lucy was his one and only—the love of his life—and he wasn't losing her without a fight. A good old-fashioned, Capriati fight. He'd storm Lucy's castle of secret romantic dreams, and lay every one of them at her feet.

Let's see if Dr. Dolittle is up to the challenge!

Brandt University, Sydney

Lucy stood in the doorway of the artificial arid house constructed for her experiment, still staring in astonishment and disbelief three days after she'd first seen the sight.

She'd done it! The trees hadn't just grown, they'd flourished; the flowers hadn't just blossomed, the apples were actually growing! Within nine months—three months ahead of schedule—the physical results were there.

"Well done, Abigail, dear. You made your theory work. You've done a very impressive job."

Lucy turned to see her mother and father behind her, with Hugh hovering in the back. All three were smiling with the approval she'd hungered for years to see. She smiled and said, "Thank you," and wondered why the sincere praise she'd craved all her life, meant so little now.

Because they damn me with faint praise. It's so cold-hearted, compared to the amazing love the Capriatis have.

Once upon a time it would have overwhelmed her, the exuberant joy of Ben's family, hugging and kissing her, when she'd shown them the success of her experiment. But not now. Not since they'd taken her into their lives and home nine months ago. They fed her, cared for her and organized to make her life easy while she worked here. They also gave her the few updates on Ben he didn't tell her himself. Their tender concern for her well-being, even their unashamed meddling in her romance with Ben, made her feel so cherished—so much a part of the Capriati family. And as she watched Papa and Mama, *Nonno* and *Nonna,* it provided living proof that the Capriati Curse became a lifetime blessing for those concerned. Love for a lifetime…

For the first time, she knew what life, and real love, was all about. Oh, Ben knew how to make her feel loved and special every day, even from seven hundred miles away. He made her feel like a princess, with seven words on paper, or on the phone.

I love you. I'm waiting for you.

"What are you going to do now?" Father asked.

She started back to the present. "Now it's time to work on the practical application—to do the field research. I'm heading out to the Northern part of Outback New South Wales to grow my apples there. It could start a whole new industry for towns that don't have large rivers, and the high irrigation of the south."

"Why not let someone else do that?" her mother said now. "Surely it's time to settle down. Hugh can't leave the city. His work is here. You've proven your point, Abigail. Your experiment worked—and a great deal of thanks for its happening at all, goes to Hugh. Now it's time to give him the support he's given you all these months."

It was weird, but it didn't even hurt that Mother gave the credit for her experiment to Hugh. She didn't even point out that she'd have completed the experiment two years ago but for his interference. Her parents weren't used to praising her, or thinking she could create a life or conduct an experiment without their help or approval. "He has?" She scratched her head. "Sorry, Hugh, I must've been so busy I didn't notice."

"Don't be flippant, dear," her mother reproved her sharply.

"Revenge is a wasted exercise." Hugh sighed. "Can't we get past this, Abigail? I've told you—you've proven yourself to me. You're a true woman of science, and fit to be my wife. Let's stop wasting time. I'm willing to marry you right away—I'll even stand the stupid dress and carriage if you want it."

She stifled the urge to laugh. Why had she thought these people omniscient? They didn't see what was right in front of their noses. So busy worrying about humanity in general, they'd forgotten to find individual humans important—and they'd lost their own humanity.

It was weird, but she didn't even feel angry at Hugh's arrogant assumption that she'd still marry him. Her anger would only be wasted on someone so self-important and blind as Hugh.

"The dress and carriage are far from stupid, Doctor Carmody. They're what Lucy wants for her wedding. A little romance at the only wedding a woman will have, isn't out of place at all. And I'm going to make sure she gets it—every single bit of it—if she'll have me."

Lucy froze, hardly daring to believe it, then, slowly, she swiveled around to the doorway.

Either she was having the most joyful hallucination of her life, or Ben was leaning against that doorway, in those molded jeans and a dark T-shirt, with that rakish, cocksure grin on his dreaming pirate's face…. "Hey, Lucy-babe. My turn to invade your domain." He marched into the arid house and propped a hip against the edge of her desk, his eyes on her face. "And I'm not leaving until I get what I want."

Oh, he'd made another fantasy come true…her conquering hero had come to rescue her! She knew she had a big grin of utter joy on her face, but she couldn't help it. "You don't have a cardigan on," she pointed out.

"I tried," he assured her with a semistraight face. "I tried really hard, babe, but you know how it goes. Could only find a pink one, and it doesn't match my pants."

If this was a dream, she hoped she'd never wake up! She knew her gaze devoured him, filled with love, and she didn't care….

"Who is this person invading the laboratory, and calling my daughter *babe?*" her mother demanded.

"You're right. I beg your pardon, Doctor Miles—and Lucy. It's a demeaning term, designed to relegate women to sexual objects. And Lucy doesn't have to be any man's object—sexual or scientific. She's her own woman, and conducts her own experiments—on plants and humans. Even me, Lucy-babe." He laughed, stood away from the desk and held out his arms to her.

"Ben…oh, Ben…" She bolted right over, jumped up into his arms, her legs around his waist and kissed him, long, deep and hard. Kissed him again and again and again, until neither of them had any breath left. "Oh, Ben, I've missed you so much," she murmured between the kisses she couldn't stop, even though she heard the outraged mutters of Hugh and her parents.

Ben snatched her as close as he could get her, kissing her all over her face, just like she was doing to him. He kissed her mouth, deep and hot and sweet, feeling as if he'd finally come in from the cold. Home and love and joy. Lucy. "Then don't miss me again," he murmured against her mouth. "Marry me, Lucy. Take my name, my life and my heart for the rest of our lives." When she didn't answer immediately he pulled back, rubbing his forehead with his hand, feeling a lump of fear fill his throat. "I know Hugh proposed—"

"Oh, that?" she laughed, nuzzling his lips. "He's done that five times since I went back to Sydney. That didn't matter. *He* doesn't matter anymore," she announced in a sunny voice, right over Hugh's indignant blustering in the background, and her parents' gasps.

The boulder in his throat stretched downward to fill his chest. "Then why did you tell me about it?"

A little silence. "Didn't you read the rest of the letter?"

"No," he confessed gruffly. "I headed straight out here to win you back."

"You missed out on a lot, then," she said gently. "Like the fact that I said I was never going to marry him. Like the fact that I feel free to choose for the first time in my life. Did you think I was sending you a 'Dear John' letter, darling?"

"Yeah," he replied without thinking—then he frowned. "Do you really think—" *She called me darling....*

"Abigail, would you mind explaining who this person is and why he would propose to you—or why you're kissing him—when you're engaged already?"

Hugh gave a loud sigh. "He's the man she was living with in Queensland. The one who won half of her prizes, and talked her out of legal action for more. So you've kept up with him secretly all these months, Abigail?"

Still clinging to Ben, Lucy turned her head. "There was no

secret about it, Hugh—it just wasn't any of your business."
She couldn't have sounded more uninterested, and Ben re-
joiced. "And I do have a mind of my own. Ben and I agreed
on stopping the legal action. After all, suing a children's charity out of greed for more than we had is pretty low."

Watching Hugh flush beet red, Ben had to hold in a laugh.
Oh, yeah, his little librarian had come into her own strength,
all right—and her family was getting their share of it.

And then he didn't have time to think, because she kissed
him again, and joy flooded every cell of his being.

"Abigail, answer my question! Why are you kissing this man
when Hugh has made it perfectly clear he wants to marry you?"

Lucy kissed him once more, as if for courage—or maybe
just because she wanted to—and then she turned again. Her
parents' faces filled with indignant wrath—but it didn't seem
to surprise her—or bother her. "Because I don't want to marry
him anymore, Mother. I don't love him—I don't think I ever
did—and frankly, I no longer respect him, either."

Lucy's father gasped. "How could you say that, Abigail?
You are very lucky to have caught his attention at all."

Ben couldn't keep quiet, not under that kind of provoca-
tion. "Professor Miles, are you aware how bad you sound
when you say things like that? Parents are usually biased in
favor of their child. They usually see the best in their children.
At least my parents do."

A scowl like human thunder came down on Lucy's father's forehead. "What business is that of yours, young man?"

Ben moved around so that he could look at Professor Miles,
face-to-face. "The business of the man who loves your daughter," he said quietly. "The man who can't imagine the rest of
his life without her. The man who knows that Doctor Carmody
is a mercenary cold fish who's unworthy of your beautiful,
intelligent, vibrant daughter. I'm unworthy, too, for that mat-

ter, but I feel like the luckiest man on earth because your daughter is in my arms."

"Ben…" With that choked word, Lucy snuggled her face into his neck. "Oh, Ben, you melt my heart…."

He lifted her face, and looked seriously into her eyes. "You don't mind that I spoke up?"

She bit her lip over the sweetest smile he'd ever seen. "Only you could stand up to my parents for me and make me feel so precious and loved instead of weak."

"You are precious to me—and definitely loved," he muttered huskily. "Add intelligent, sweet, adorable and beautiful to that list and you're about right."

"I love you," she whispered, and pure happiness flooded him. She'd finally said it. She loved him…she *loved* him!

Lucy's father said sharply, "Young man, you may think this is the way to carry on in a scientific laboratory, but—" Then he frowned, looking at Ben closely. "Do I know you? Your face seems familiar."

Ben looked into the face of his future father-in-law. "I did premed classes with you six years ago, sir—and the deeper study of endocrinology was never so fascinating. I'm Ben Capriati. You're currently lecturing my brother Joe."

Ben held in the grin as Christopher Miles's tirade ended with those magical, respectful words. "Capriati—of course! The scholarship boy. Coleman and Larkins in human pathology said they'd never had a better assistant!"

Ben did smile now; it seemed safe. "I'm glad to hear it, sir, since those jobs got me through two years of my college life, and got me out of waiting tables and tending bar at night."

Professor Miles frowned. "You turned down three offers to go into research with Sydney University, didn't you?"

Ben nodded, still carrying Lucy, her legs wrapped around his waist—and he wasn't planning on putting her down, maybe not for the next ten or twenty years if at all possible. "I wanted to go into general practice, sir. I work in the country now."

Both the Mileses looked at him with deep respect. "Helping the country folk without the Flying Doctor?" Mary Miles asked.

He nodded. "For the next five years at least." He glanced at Lucy, who smiled at him with such trusting love, his heart and gut flipped. "It's a fairly arid area. It's perfect for the practical application of Lucy's apple experiment. If she wants it, I've bought a two hundred acre allotment of land outside town. It's already got a lot of the types of saltbush and weed she needs, occurring naturally. It hasn't been cleared in over a decade, so the trees can be transplanted right in."

"I've loosened the soil around the roots already," she murmured, her eyes shining. "I can transport them in a week."

He smiled into those shining Irish eyes. "Marry me?"

She kissed his nose. "Well, all right…but I'm only coming for the food." Her eyes twinkled. "And the free land, of course."

Laughing, it was his turn to bury his face in her neck. "Ah, Lucy, what you do to me," he muttered huskily.

After a tender, whispered, "I hope so," she looked up at her parents. "Mother, Father, I'm glad you know and respect Ben for the man he is, but it wouldn't have mattered if you didn't. I'm going to marry him, because I'm madly in love with him."

"Well, obviously," Mary Miles said with a lifted eyebrow. "I can't help but confess to some minor disappointment in the way you've gone about this, Abigail, but you're an adult now, and your marriage is your decision." She turned to Monkey-boy, standing morose behind her. "I am sorry, Hugh, but she has made her decision—and it is a wise choice for her career, since Ben works in the area she needs to be."

Hugh sighed, and gave Lucy a sad, puzzled look. "What did I do to deserve this defection, Abigail?"

Lucy grinned at him. "Nothing, Hugh," she replied blandly. "Nothing at all. Three or four long years of nothing."

Ben chuckled. "Give him pepper, Lucy-babe," he whispered in her ear, and she giggled aloud. After a foul glance at Ben, Hugh stalked out the door, the Greek God effect ruined by the childish sulk marring his face, and by his slamming the door, hard. "Most unscientific of him, don't you think?" Ben whispered again.

Lucy chuckled. "Oh, I've *missed* you, Ben…nobody makes me laugh like you do."

"So when is this wedding?" his future mother-in-law asked before they could kiss again.

"I don't want to wait a day longer than I have to. The wedding will happen as soon as the license comes through," Ben answered, cuddling Lucy close. "I applied for it this morning, just in case, so a month and a day from now. Do you want to get married here or in Monilough?" he asked Lucy.

"Where our lives are going to be," she replied, her whole face glowing with happiness. "My friends from here are happy to take a weekend off to head north. And I know your family will make the trek up there, since we've been collaborating on wedding plans for the past nine months," she admitted with a grin, "and they've had Father Bonatti and the whole family on standby since I told them I could transplant my trees. Ask all your friends to come, Ben. I want them to be my friends, too."

"They will be," he replied huskily. "They'll all love you, just like my family love you. But they'd better not love you like I do. You're mine," he mock growled, and she giggled again, glowing. Man, he loved her laugh; he hadn't realized how much he'd missed hearing it.

Christopher Miles frowned. "A month isn't enough notice for us to get leave, Abigail. If you'll wait six months or so? I have classes to conduct, and practicals at the hospital, and your mother—"

She shook her head. "No, Father. For once I'm not going to wait for your convenience. I've always put your wants and needs before mine, and it's time you came through for me. I told you three months ago this wedding would happen as soon as my theoretical experiment was finalized."

Ben chuckled softly. "Nothing like being sure, is there?"

She grinned and whispered, "With your family planning the whole thing for me, updating me on your plans while they took care of me the past nine months, why not? I've even taken religious instruction for the wedding."

Moved at her words, he simply mouthed *I love you,* and she mouthed it back before turning back to her parents.

"I've waited long enough for my wedding, Father, and so has Ben. If you can't come, that's okay—I'll send you photos."

Her parents blinked, obviously stunned by her refusal to put her life on permanent hold for their convenience. "We'll have to discuss this, obviously, dear. And try to organize for time off," Professor Miles said. He hesitated, glancing at Ben. "Would you both like to come home for dinner tonight?"

"Thank you—but tomorrow, Father," Lucy said softly. "Ben's parents haven't seen him in months. They'll want to see him tonight."

Her parents hesitated, nodded, and with strange, unsure smiles, left the arid house, leaving Ben and Lucy alone.

She smiled after them. "I don't know how they'll take the idea that the marriage is going to be performed by Father Bonatti. I thought maybe I should keep that back until they're used to other things first."

Ben stared at her, thrilled and proud and touched by how much she'd done to prove her love to him, to show the strength of her commitment to being part of his family. "Are you sure you want to do that? If my family pushed this on you—"

"They didn't," she replied emphatically. "I was the one to ask about it. I love them, Ben. I want them to be happy." She smiled. "And they are, even though it's in the hall, not the church. Papa and *Nonno* made sure I got to all my instruction classes with Father Bonatti so that he'd agree to marry us." There was a touch more anxiety in her smile now. "I hope you don't mind having the wedding in the community hall? I'm happy to be married by Father Bonatti and have ongoing instruction, but I guess my training is still there. I'm not ready for the full nuptial thing in the church. Father Bonatti was fine with that—though he had to do some fast talking to the local bishop—but are you okay with it?"

"Are you kidding? I'd marry you in a pagan ritual in a cave if that's what you wanted." From his jacket pocket, he pulled out the velvet box he'd obsessively carried since he'd bought it. He got the lovely, dark fire opal ring encrusted with diamonds, and slid it onto her finger, seeing her wide-eyed delight at his choice. "Sometimes it scares me, how much I love you," he confessed gruffly.

Her eyes misty with joy, she whispered back, "The only thing that would scare me is if you ever stopped loving me."

He kissed her nose. "Then you never need to be scared again in your life."

"Ben." The word was all choked up. "Oh, Ben, I love you so much!"

The declaration filled him with such joy, what else could he do but kiss her? "Then let's go see the family, and get everything ready for our wedding. I can't wait to bring you home, and have you to myself," he said, husky with need.

"Me, too." She nuzzled his neck.

"I hope you got the tiara you liked?"

She nodded, smiling. "Of course. I knew you'd want me to."

"And the horse-drawn carriage?"

"I think we'd both prefer to ride away to our honeymoon on Jan." Her face glowed with newfound confidence, with the maturity of a love returned, throwing out the less important things—making him so proud of her, it hurt.

He buried his face in her throat, hating to say it. "Lucy, we can't go away for a honeymoon. I've already had these days off, and I doubt I'll get any more for another six months. I didn't have time to arrange for someone to take over my practice, and though Joe will be there, he's not legally qualified until next year."

She kissed his hair. "It's all right, Ben. We can ride home, then. I'll be happy as long as I'm with you."

"I know how much you want a honeymoon. I arranged for us to have seven days at a bed-and-breakfast luxury cabin at Charlie Dobson's farm outside town. That way I'm there if anyone needs me, and we get time alone. It's stocked up with food and everything else we'll need, so we don't need to leave for the whole week." He searched her face. "I know it's not enough, but I swear, as soon as I organize a locum, we'll take that trip to Fiji we won, or anywhere you want to go."

"Perfect. It sounds perfect." She caressed his face. "Do you think I mind where we are, Ben, so long as we're together? I just want to be alone with you—to make love with you," she confessed huskily.

She knew. She understood. How did he ever get so lucky? The day she stormed into his house had been the best possible day of his life...until the day she became his wife. "Do you know what you do to me, Lucy?" he asked raggedly.

She wrapped her arms tight around him, drawing him closer. "I hope so," she whispered, "because I know what you do to me..."

The kiss, while sweet and tender, slowly grew in intensity, in passion—and in love. Finally, finally the lovely little Irish dreamer who had taken his heart in a day, would be his, his love forever.

Much later, breathing hard, he made himself stop. A month wasn't so long to wait—and he wanted that first night to be perfect. Though he'd never considered himself a traditional man, he was glad that his first time with Lucy would be as husband and wife. "Let's go and give the family the good news. They're waiting to hear." He smiled as she climbed down with obvious reluctance. He held out a hand to her, and she put hers in it…just as she would for the rest of their lives.

Epilogue

A month later

Ben stood waiting at the end of the aisle for his bride. Joe, Marco and Jack were beside him, joking about his becoming another victim to the dreaded Curse.

He didn't care; he was too happy. He knew when their turn came, they'd understand that what happened to the Capriati men was nobody's curse. He blessed that cranky old wise-woman, for helping him find his soul mate in the unlikeliest place. Finding true love when he least expected it.

A rustle of sound at the end of the hall made him turn—and he caught his breath. In the entrance bedecked with flowers, Lucy stood behind his sister, Sofie. She looked so vivid and sweet and lovely in white tulle and old-fashioned lace, smiling at him through Mama's filmy old wedding veil—and so radiant with joy and love for him, he ached.

Like a tender benediction, "Unchained Melody" began its haunting, old-fashioned seduction of love from the jukebox n the corner. Smiling, Sofie started the traditional march; then, flanked by Papa and *Nonno,* Lucy began her journey down the aisle to him.

He felt his hands and knees shaking, but he managed to stay upright, wearing a damn-fool happy grin. Tenderness and pride filled him and overflowed. His little librarian had come into her own. She'd made her dreams come to life—and his—by remaining true to herself, and refusing to settle for second best.

When Lucy gave Sofie her bouquet to hold, Sofie hugged her. "Who gives this woman to this man?"

Papa and *Nonno* turned to Professor Miles, sitting in the front row beside his wife who was quietly mopping tears. They'd only come at the last moment, too late to play a part in the wedding. Lucy had insisted on keeping Papa and Nonno as those who would give her away; it had meant so much more to them, or so she'd thought.

But Papa and *Nonno* held out their hands to her father, offering him a choice—and a chance. After a moment, Christopher Miles got to his feet and joined them, taking Lucy's hand in his. All three men said together, "We do."

Then her father lifted the veil, and gently kissed her. "I'm proud of you—Lucy," he said quietly. "You've been a good daughter to us. I'm only sorry we didn't tell you more often."

Lucy's eyes glittered with happy tears as she kissed him back. "Thank you, Father...."

Papa and *Nonno* kissed her, and replaced the veil, then *Nonno* put her hand into Ben's. As they twined fingers, the whole family broke out into exuberant, spontaneous applause.

Yes, Lucy had become a Capriati, with all the fierce, loving loyalty it entailed...and Ben couldn't ask for a better wedding present—except Lucy herself.

Half an hour later, Father Bonatti said the words he'd feared would never come to him outside his dreams. "Good folk, I'd like to present to you Ben and Lucy Capriati, husband and wife." He winked at Ben. "Go ahead and kiss her, son."

Trembling all over now, he lifted her veil, and looked deep into her eyes before he kissed her with all the love he had. "Thank you, Lucy," he whispered against her mouth. "You once offered to make my fantasy come true. Today, you did."

She smiled up at him, misty and soft and radiant. "You're the love of my life. I hope I always make your dreams come true."

"It was worth waiting for, to have this day."

She shook her head. "Not just this day, Ben. For all the days and nights we'll have together. For the children we'll bring into the world. For a life where we're truly a needed part of the community. It was all worth the wait." She added, with a naughty twinkle in her eyes, "And the fantasies aren't over yet, buster. I still haven't played Marilyn. There's one or two very special outfits waiting for us in that honeymoon cabin. I have some fabulous ideas…"

"But not tonight," he said softly. "Tonight is just for Ben and Lucy."

"Yes. Just us—and nothing between," she whispered.

He kissed her again, with growing hunger and passion, then, interrupted by Jack's good-natured ribbing about waiting until they were alone, they laughed and turned around to hugs and kisses and laughter, sharing their special evening with the people who loved them best.

But the night, like every night from now on, would be theirs alone.

* * * * *

SILHOUETTE *Romance*®

Don't miss

DADDY IN THE MAKING
by Sharon De Vita

Silhouette Romance #1743

A daddy is all six-year-old Emma DiRosa wants.
And when handsome Michael Gallagher gets
snowbound with the little girl and her single
mother Angela, Emma thinks she's found
the perfect candidate. Now, she just needs
to get Angela and Michael to realize
what was meant to be!

Available November 2004

If you enjoyed what you just read,
then we've got an offer you can't resist!

Take 2 bestselling
love stories FREE!

Plus get a FREE surprise gift!

SILHOUETTE *Romance*®

COMING NEXT MONTH

#1742 RICH MAN, POOR BRIDE—Linda Goodnight
In a Fairy Tale World…
Ruthie Ellsworthy Fernandez is determined to steer clear of gorgeous military physician Diego Vargas and his wandering ways. Ruthie wants roots, a home and a family more than anything, and though Diego's promises are tempting, they're only temporary—aren't they?

#1743 DADDY IN THE MAKING—Sharon De Vita
Danger is Michael Gallagher's middle name. But when he comes to a rural Wisconsin inn to unwind and lay low, beautiful innkeeper Angela DiRosa and her adorable daughter charm their way into his life. And soon Michael is finding that risking his heart is the most dangerous adventure of all.

#1744 THE BOWEN BRIDE—Nicole Burnham
Can a wedding dress made from magical fabric guarantee a lasting marriage? That's what Katie Schmidt wonders about her grandmother's special thread. And when handsome single father Jared Porter walks into Katie's bridal shop, she wonders if the magic is strong enough to weave this wonderful man into her life for good.

#1745 A WHIRLWIND…MAKEOVER—Nancy Lavo
Maddie Sinclair is a walking disaster! But when she needs a date to her high school reunion, her friend Dan Willis uses his photographer's eye to transform her from mousy to magnificent. With her new looks, Maddie's turning heads…especially Dan's.